PRAISE FOR *SARA LOST AND FOUND*

★ "Sara's story will tug at heartstrings; readers will cheer for her to succeed, for she is a heroine in the style of *The Great Gilly Hopkins*. . . . This book is a must for middle school readers." —*VOYA*, starred review

"Castleman uses her own experiences in the American foster-care system to inspire the trials through which Sara goes. The first-person, present-tense style lets readers live through Sara's thoughts and . . . pack an emotional punch." —*Booklist*

"Written from debut novelist Castleman's childhood experience of adoption from an orphanage, this title offers much fodder for discussion." —*Kirkus Reviews*

SARA LOST AND FOUND

VIRGINIA CASTLEMAN

Aladdin

New York London Toronto Sydney New Delhi

This book is a work of fiction. Any references to historical events, real people, or real places are used fictitiously. Other names, characters, places, and events are products of the author's imagination, and any resemblance to actual events or places or persons, living or dead, is entirely coincidental.

ALADDIN
An imprint of Simon & Schuster Children's Publishing Division
1230 Avenue of the Americas, New York, New York 10020
First Aladdin paperback edition February 2017
Text copyright © 2014 by Virginia Castleman
Originally published in 2014 by Archway Publishing.
Cover photograph copyright © 2016 by Jamie Heiden
Also available in an Aladdin hardcover edition.
All rights reserved, including the right of reproduction
in whole or in part in any form.
ALADDIN and related logo are registered trademarks of Simon & Schuster, Inc.
For information about special discounts for bulk purchases,
please contact Simon & Schuster Special Sales
at 1-866-506-1949 or business@simonandschuster.com.
The Simon & Schuster Speakers Bureau can bring authors to your live event.
For more information or to book an event contact the Simon & Schuster Speakers Bureau
at 1-866-248-3049 or visit our website at www.simonspeakers.com.
Cover designed by Dan Potash
Interior designed by Mike Rosamilia
The text of this book was set in Scala OT.
Manufactured in the United States of America 0117 OFF
2 4 6 8 10 9 7 5 3 1
The Library of Congress has cataloged the hardcover edition as follows:
Castleman, Virginia.
Sara lost and found / by Virginia Castleman.
p. cm.
Summary: When their mother abandons them and their father
ends up in jail again, ten-year-old Sara and her mentally troubled
sister are thrust back into the foster care system.
[1. Foster home care—Fiction. 2. Sisters—Fiction.
3. Emotional problems—Fiction.] I. Title.
PZ7.C268739Sar 2016
[Fic]—dc23
2015004222
ISBN 978-1-4814-3871-1 (hc)
ISBN 978-1-4814-3872-8 (pbk)
ISBN 978-1-4814-3873-5 (eBook)

To the hundreds of thousands of children in foster care in the United States, and to the foster parents and adoptive parents who raise and care for them

CHAPTER 1

SOMETIMES THERE'S A TUG-OF-WAR INSIDE OF ME.
My head says one thing. My stomach says another. Like
yesterday, when I stole a roll of paper towels from the
7-Eleven around the corner. My head said, *Don't*. My
stomach said, *Do*.

So I did.

I stole.

And yeah, paper towels might seem like a strange
thing to steal. I mean, I could have stolen some candy,
or crackers or something. But paper towels last longer
than food. A roll of paper towels can feed me and my
sister, Anna, for a whole week—sometimes more.

I know my name is Sara Rose Olson. I know what

empty feels like. And I know I should feel bad for stealing. But I don't. Last night, waiting for Daddy to come home, I ripped off pieces of paper towel, wadded them up, chewed the paper balls soft and slow, and swallowed. I felt better. I gave some to Anna. She sat cross-legged on the floor next to me. We didn't have to talk about it. We just ate. I pictured myself biting into a juicy hamburger. I know Anna was picturing her favorite—hot dogs.

Eating paper towels is the secret way I trick my stomach into thinking it's been fed. It works, too. By the time Anna and I'd eaten only half a square of paper towel, our stomachs quit making those whiny noises. And after eating one towel each, we both felt better.

Tonight I'm not awake because I'm hungry. I have a stomach full of paper towel. Tonight what's keeping me awake is the wind. It's whipping around like it needs to get somewhere *fast*.

I look around. Spidery shadows dance on the walls. A *skit, skit* across the floorboards draws my eyes to the dark hallway. At first I think the sound is rain pattering down instead of little rat claws skittering, but when their tiny feet hit the paper on the floor, the sound changes to a muffled scuffle. Rain doesn't sound like that.

Then a different noise makes me listen even harder. It sounds like someone scratching against the window. My whole body turns cold. I lie frozen on the bed, too scared to look, but then I slowly sit up, squeeze my eyes shut, open them, and squint against the darkness. The window slowly starts looking like a window, instead of a big, dark hole in the wall.

I look through the dark pane, heart pounding. No prowler. Just the low branches of a tree scraping against the glass. I lie back on the mattress slowly. It's got some small rips, and hard springs press against my back. I try to get my breath to slow down.

I've been jumpy like this ever since last year, when I turned nine. A couple of days after my birthday, Mama took off, leaving a hole in me so big she might just as well have died. Daddy, Anna, and I weren't the only things she left behind. Mama left a letter, too, and a picture. I hid them, afraid Daddy would tear them up or throw them away like everything else of Mama's that he tossed out after she left us. The letter and picture are almost the only things of Mama that Anna and I have left. Just thinking about Daddy finding them sends heat through me that warms me up. He'll be so mad I hid them if he ever finds out.

"That woman is plumb crazy," he'd tell us. But then I think of what Mama said to me once, and I feel cold again. It wasn't crazy that made Mama run off. It was me.

"Every time I look at you, I see him."

I know the "him" Mama was talking about was Daddy. I can't help thinking that if only I looked different, Mama wouldn't have run away. Now Daddy's gone too.

Not gone-gone, like Mama.

Just gone.

Daddy disappears every once in a while, but he always comes back. It's been longer this time, though, and Anna and I are more scared than a pair of cats in a room full of rocking chairs.

Daddy's a singer and drummer in a band called Stix and Stonz. Stones is the last name of two other guys in the band. They call Daddy "Stix" because he's skinny, and because he plays the drums. Sometimes at night I lie awake and hear him drumming in his room. *Tat-tat-tat*, like rain on a tin roof, like the top of a shed Anna and I once hid in. I listen hard to hear the sound in my thoughts. Normally, it brings Daddy closer, but tonight my thoughts won't work right.

The scratching noises don't scare me anymore, but I'm still cold. I roll onto my side and peek at Anna, whose face, for once, doesn't look all twisted. It's good to see her sleeping so hard and not waking up because of horrible nightmares, the noisy wind, scratchy trees, or skittering rats.

A couple of nights ago, Anna and I buried one we found in the alley. Even though it was dead, its bright little beady eyes glowed in the moonlight. The rat couldn't have been dead long. Its fur was still soft, yet it lay there like a clump of loosened dirt.

We lined a box with soft leaves. The coffin was a shoe box we'd saved full of treasures, including the picture of Mama, which I took out and put in my jacket. Then we gave the rat a name. No one should die without a name. I wanted to name it Sid because I thought that was a great name for a rat, but Anna gave it another name.

"Hope it's not dead."

"It is," I said.

"Hope we can fix it."

"We can't."

"Bury Hope," she murmured.

And we did. We buried Hope with all the love we could muster.

The ceremony was a short one. Anna scooped dirt over the box while I sang a good-bye song I made up right on the spot. When the last scoop of dirt was patted down, we made a ring of small rocks around the lumpy mound. Then we marched back to the house, sad for Hope but happy that we could send the rat on its new journey in a nice box with two somebodies missing it.

I climb out of bed, telling myself with each step that everything's going to be okay. The wooden floor is cold and sends tiny shivers up my legs. I walk faster. I try to pull the window all the way shut, but it won't budge. A chilly breeze swirls around my nightshirt.

A movement on the glass makes me jump. My heart beats faster. *Is someone outside peeking in after all?*

When I look again, I see that it's only me in the glass and feel silly at being scared of my own face. Seeing myself in the glass makes me feel better—like I'm not alone.

Sometimes reflections look like they're supposed

to—color and all. Other times, or at other angles, I can only make out shadows. I lean close to the cold glass for a better look. In the shadows, my hair looks inky black. I look different with such dark hair. My hair is really brown like toast. In the reflection, my eyes are round, black circles, like holes in a skull, instead of sky blue. I remember Daddy saying that when God made me, He put a piece of that blue sky in my eyes so I would see great things.

I lean against the dusty sill, hugging my arms around me. Sometimes the dark feels warm and safe, other times cold and scary. Still, one thing never changes about the dark: I can always count on it to be there. I just wish Anna and I didn't have to be alone in it so much. I cross the room and crawl back into bed, roll up into a tight ball, and tuck my feet under me—forcing myself not to snuggle up against my sister for warmth. I'm sure that if even one cold toe touches Anna, she'll wake up with a jolt, swinging her arms, and she needs to sleep.

Even though she's two years older than me, I sometimes feel like her older sister. I have to watch over her, especially when Daddy's gone. Which makes me wonder, *Where can he be? What if something bad has happened to him?* I'm thinking a car crash, but he doesn't have a car—though he could have gotten mugged. I count the marks on the wall. It's been seven nights since we saw him last.

My eyes sting from tears, but I hold them in. Crying doesn't bring him back. At least, it never has before.

I wrap my arm around my stuffed black-and-white cat and listen to Anna breathe. Daddy said the toy looked more like a cow than a cat, so I named it Cowwy. Daddy found Cowwy lying in the street, dirty, missing a button for an eye. He brought him home and gave him to me for my birthday. Cowwy still has only one eye, but we cleaned him up.

I roll over and look at the hole where the door is, hoping Daddy will suddenly fill it, but the doorway is empty and the hall is dark. He'll come back. He promised.

I close my eyes and picture Daddy up on the stage, half hidden in smoke. Fat people, skinny people, happy people, sad people—all kinds fill the room. The lights dim and the crowd settles. Daddy sits behind his drums in a big black felt cowboy hat, jeans, a faded denim shirt, and scuffed black boots. He closes his eyes and sings a tune about a love gone wrong. His sad songs always make me want to cry.

I start to sing one of his songs in my head when a soft thump, like a door closing, jars my thoughts back to the room, the shadows, and the noises that are right and wrong. Something about this noise doesn't sound right. I sit up in bed and listen hard. Maybe Daddy's home after all! He does that sometimes. Slipping in when he isn't drinking, thumping and bumping to his room when he is. But this wasn't thumping and bumping. This was just one soft thump.

"Daddy?" I try to keep my voice low so I don't wake Anna, but loud enough to carry into the next room.

"Daddy, is that you?"

No answer.

I roll from the mattress, cross the room, and peek out the door. Shadows dance, but nothing else in the next room moves. Something about the air smells different—sweeter, maybe—but I can't place it. I pause at Daddy's bedroom door. No light. No sound. I peek around the doorway at the mattress on the floor, hoping to see a familiar lump under the sheets. No lump. No Daddy.

"Is that you?" I whisper again, knowing no answer

9

will come but still hoping one might. I go back and flop down on the bed, wanting to feel the heat from Daddy's body on the mattress, telling me he'd just been there— like maybe he'd gotten up to go to the bathroom. But the mattress is cold.

I grab one corner of the sheet and start twisting it into a rope. It's a game I play with myself. I call it the hugging game. When the sheet is fully twisted, I wrap a rope-hug around me as tight as I can. The hug feels good, almost like Daddy is here, holding me in his big arms. The mattress is still—not gently rising and falling like Daddy's chest. No sound of his heartbeat inside the pillow against my ear—just the faint smell of smoke from Daddy's hair and skin.

My throat tightens, and my mouth twitches like it does right before I'm going to cry. I bite my lip hard to chase the tears away.

"Daddy home?" Anna's voice startles me. For one thing, she hardly ever talks, and for another, I thought she was asleep. But here she is, leaning sleepily against the doorway.

"Not yet." I undo the rope-hug and pat the mattress beside me.

Anna shuffles across the room and sits on the edge of the bed. I hear tiny snaps as she bites her fingernails. She's lost somewhere in her head. We sit together in the dark, thinking about things, when suddenly three loud raps on the front door make us jump.

I reach out and cling to Anna.

CHAPTER 2

THREE MORE SHARP KNOCKS RATTLE THE WALLS.
I grip Anna's hand tightly, afraid to let go. At first I figure that's why she starts to cry, but, really, she's more
scared than I am.

"Shhh, it's okay." I try to sound like I mean it, even
though I'm not feeling one bit like anything's okay. "It
might be the wind knocking."

A man's voice drifts into the room. "Sara?"

Even Anna knows the wind doesn't talk, let alone
say my name. It isn't Daddy's voice, either.

"I'll go see who it is." I pry my fingers free from
Anna's grip and start for the door. Anna follows, close
as a shadow behind me.

When I get to the front door, I press my ear against it. The wood is cold and hard. Still, I know anger can come through that wood and splinter it in one easy blow. No bad words. No pounding fists on the door. Just another loud *knock, knock, knock.*

"Who is it?" I put on my bravest voice.

"It's the police, Sara. Open the door."

I look at Anna, remembering how Daddy always said not to open the door for anyone. Anna looks scared enough to crumple. I stretch up on my tiptoes, cup my hand to her ear, and whisper, "He could be trying to trick us into opening the door—saying he's the police when really he isn't." But another voice, a woman's, sounds familiar.

"Sara, dear, it's Ruth Craig from Child Protective Services. We need you to open the door, sweetie."

I remember her. She's the caseworker who took us to the Cottages right after Mama left. The Cottages are a place where kids who've been separated from their parents stay until the judge at the court decides what to do with them. Daddy had gone out drinking and time kind of got away from him. But he came back and got us within a week.

"Where's my dad?" I ask, finding Anna's hand in the dark.

The woman's voice comes through the wood again. "Your dad had to go to a special place for a while, Sara, but he wanted us to come and get you."

I know the special place she's talking about is jail.

"What did he do?" I glance at Anna's face, lost in the shadows.

"He got into a bad fight at the club where his band was playing," Mrs. Craig explains. "Sara, please. I know you and Anna must be hungry. Wouldn't you like something to eat?"

They'll try to trick you with food, Daddy said. *Don't open the door.* So even though the thought of food makes my stomach rumble, I gently tug on Anna's hand and lead her into the kitchen, pointing to the back door. I press a finger to my lips.

"Run away?" Anna's eyes widen. I nod solemnly. Even though it hadn't worked every time we'd tried it before, it seemed like the only thing to do.

"Open the door, Sara!" The man's voice grows louder.

Anna gives me a panicked look and then races to our room and returns moments later with Abby, her doll, and Cowwy. "Can't leave them," she murmurs. She's right. I hug Cowwy and grab my jacket. Something falls out of the torn lining.

Mama's letter!

I pick it up and stuff it back into my jacket, then grab Anna's hand.

Usually when we open the back screen door, it makes an awful *screech*, wild and shrill. But tonight, with the wind wailing, the screech isn't much louder than a squeak. The door closes behind us with a soft *thoop*. I tighten my grip on Anna's hand and give it a tug. Crouched down, we cross the weed-choked backyard, past dented trash cans and a stack of old tires covered with giant spiderwebs.

The alley is no more than one car wide and has deep tire tracks on either side. We sneak past nine houses— four on one side, five on the other, most with peeling paint.

When we finally reach the end of the alley, we turn the corner onto Elm Street, slip past the shoe store, and stop in front of Big Eddie's Bakery. The sweet, toasty smell of doughnuts makes my stomach bark with hunger. I breathe in deep and swallow, mad at myself for not remembering to grab a piece of paper towel before we sneaked out of the house. I could have stuffed it in my pocket. Big Ed, as everyone calls him, is a fat, sweaty man who looks more black than brown against his big white apron. I wait until he pulls a tray of fresh-baked doughnuts from the oven—his back is turned—and then tug on Anna's arm.

"Where we going?" Her voice shivers. I know she's scared. We duck behind a Dumpster that smells both sweet and rotten-trash sour and wait for cars to go by. One slows down. It's a police car with a bright light searching the sides of the street. I feel Anna stiffen when the light hits the Dumpster. We curl up so tight that my head almost touches my toes.

He must not see us because he drives right by, and I let out a deep breath. I tap on Anna's back and motion for her to go. She doesn't move. I tug her hand harder, and she tips over.

"Come on, Anna. They'll catch us if we don't get out of here."

Finally, she uncurls and stands up.

"Which way?"

"This way." I make my voice as strong as a whisper can sound. Anna relaxes and follows, this time without holding us back.

CHAPTER 3

RIDING DOWN A STREET WITH A CASEWORKER
driving us to a new foster home is a lot different from
walking it in the dark. At first, everything looks like I
remember it. I guide Anna this way and that to avoid
dogs that might give us away, but then we hit streets I
don't know. I turn down one that looks quieter than the
others. Someone yells from an open window. Behind
us, a group of men stand around a car, smoking and
blasting music. Another car drives up, and everyone
starts yelling.

One of the streetlights is burned out, and we duck
into the shadows. When the men start throwing fists
in the air and shouting bad words, I force Anna to

cross the street to get us as far away from them as I can. I drag her up close to the houses so we can't be seen so easily from the street. Bushes reach out and scratch us. Even the ones with flowers on them aren't friendly at night.

"Daddy there?"

I look back. Anna looks too.

"No. Daddy's not with them."

That I know. Just like I know Daddy's at the same place these guys are going to be if the fighting gets any worse. But I don't tell her that.

"Come on, Anna. Don't look back."

After at least a thousand steps through dirt, rocks, weeds, and grass, we reach a clearing.

Anna points excitedly. "The fountain!" She races for it.

We call it "the fountain" even though there's no water in it. I don't want to drag Anna away, but the statue is out in the open, and someone might see us. "Let's go to the Silvermans'," I whisper.

Her eyes light up. "Ben and Rachel!" Even though she's excited, I have to peel her from the statue.

"Come on, Anna. We'll freeze to death out here if

we don't get going." My legs are already stiff with cold, and my nightshirt does little to keep the wind from wrapping around my legs. We pass by a store window. A plastic girl smiles out at us. She's wearing a white pair of pants with a blue-and-white top.

As we round the corner, I think about her, wishing we could trade places for the night. I picture myself in her clothes, sitting at the window, watching people pass by all day, smiling away, hoping one of them will be Daddy or Mama coming to take us home.

Ahead, I spot the gate and relax a little. I'd know that gate anywhere. I remember it because it doesn't open to anything. Maybe a long time ago it did, but now it stands at the edge of a field, covered in creepy vines that come back to life in the spring. Daddy said that it probably opened onto a cemetery at one time, but the cemetery is gone. I didn't know cemeteries could go anywhere.

Anna and I slip past the gate and, crouching down, start across the dark, weedy field. Anna's grip tightens.

"Hear that?" She moves up so close behind me that she steps on my heel.

I wince. "There's nothing to hear," I tell her,

quickening my pace. "See that elephant tree over there by that rusted-out car?" It was a sycamore. I know because Ben taught me about trees, and sycamore trunks are as big around as elephants. Their patchy bark reminds me of elephant hide, even though I've never actually touched an elephant. And their leaves are silky soft, like I imagine elephant ears to be.

They have dangly fruit with prickly things covering them that hurt when you step on them. So, as much as I would like to go and pat the trunk of the elephant sycamore, I make a wide circle around it, dragging Anna behind me.

"Ben's tree!" Anna squeals. Ben taught us both about trees. He says we can learn a lot from them, like how if they don't grow deep roots, a big wind can blow them over like dominoes. Anna clearly remembers that the sycamore marks where Ben and Rachel's street starts.

It's not easy walking through prickly weeds in bare feet. I try not to think about the burning scratches on my legs or how I can't even feel my toes anymore. Even Anna doesn't complain.

In the moonlight, I see another tree, an oak, beside

the sycamore. I slow down to take it all in, and something moves. Something big. Anna sees it too, and stiffens.

All I can think is that maybe the cemetery didn't go away after all, and that maybe a ghost or something is mad because we didn't knock on the gate before sneaking in, or maybe—

A fire burns brightly in a nearby garbage can. I see them then, gathered around the fire. Some are wrapped in coats, others in blankets, all huddled together.

"Who's there?" Anna asks.

I can feel her breath on my cheek. I know the shadows are homeless people, just like me and Anna at the moment, and they are trying to stay warm. They have a new family now: each other.

"They're the forgotten ones," I whisper, widening our path around them.

"Like us," Anna says, straining to look at them.

Her words cut deep. Daddy wouldn't forget us. He's locked up. That's why he's not here. "Let's go this way."

"Get warm?" Anna pulls on my hand. I know she's looking at the fires. Before I can answer, a sound comes out of her that makes my hair stand up. It's the sound that fear makes when it takes over your whole body. I glance back and see a dark streak racing right at us.

"Run!" I pull hard on Anna's hand, but she freezes.

"Come on, Anna!" I jerk hard on her arm as a dog closes in.

"Princess!" A man's voice cuts through the darkness. The voice jerks the dog back like a leash has been pulled, and instead of coming after us it runs back to the circle of shadows gathered around the fire.

"Are you okay?" I turn to Anna, surprised by what I see. She's smiling! Or maybe the muscles in her face have just frozen with fear. "Anna?" I wrap an arm around her and guide her toward the street.

She walks stiffly, all the while grinning that strange grin. "Princess?" Her voice cracks.

"If that was the princess, I don't want to see the prince," I whisper, hugging her. She lets out a sound that I've learned is a laugh and looks back at the dog. A new look comes over her face, like maybe she sees herself in it.

Her biting self, that is.

Anna just can't help it. If someone scares her bad enough, she bites.

When I look up, I see familiar street lamps—the ones that line Ben and Rachel's street, and my heart swells in my chest. The Silvermans' house is still a long way away, but at least I know we're going down the right street, and that makes my feet hurt a whole lot less.

"Keep up, Anna." In my mind, I see myself letting her go—leaving her to find her own way. But then my body heats up with shame. What am I thinking? Leave Anna alone? She needs me. And what about the promise I made to her? The promise that no matter what, nothing and no one will ever pull us apart.

I don't like to think about the last time Mama ran away. It was a Thursday. I remember because my birthday was on Monday, and she left a few days later. Our caseworker picked us up from school.

"Where's Mama?" I had asked her.

"Let's talk in the car."

"Talk in the car" meant she didn't want everyone else hearing, so that told me that whatever news she had wasn't good.

After Anna and I were buckled in, she put her arm up over the top of the seat and cranked her neck around to look at us.

Even though it happened a year ago, I remember her answer like she was saying it to me today. "Your mama was picked up in another state for DUI and damage to another person's vehicle."

"What's DUI?" It didn't sound like anything too bad. ABC, DUI.

"It stands for 'driving under the influence.' She drove after she had been drinking and ran into someone's car."

Mrs. Craig paused, letting the information sink in. But something about what she said refused to sink.

"Wait. You said Mama was picked up in another state? Why is Mama in another state?"

Our caseworker sighed. "I don't know all the details, Sara, but since your father has his own set of challenges and can't come home, you and Anna will need to go stay with some temporary families until your parents are free to come and get you."

I won't say she tricked me. She did say "families," not "family." I should have been sharper. I should have picked up on it. But I didn't, and for the first time, Anna and I were ripped apart and placed in two different homes. Sometimes one family that already has kids can't take on two more, even for a short time. That's what Mrs. Craig said, anyway.

It was the longest month of my life, not knowing how Anna was getting on, and not being able to talk to her. Most kids at school have cell phones, but you can't eat or wear a cell phone, so it wasn't something we could afford to get, and with the caseworkers being so busy, it's left up to the foster parents to arrange the phone calls.

After that awful month, when we got to go back home, Mama never talked about why she had been in another state, and I never asked. And something about Anna wasn't right. It was as if something broke inside her. I tried to get her to talk about it, but she'd just growl and draw her shoulders up almost to her ears, head back, arms bent at her sides, with her hands clenched into fists, looking like a cornered animal about to attack.

What I did see before she hid them were the raw, red marks on her arm. "What are those?"

She wouldn't say. She just crossed her good arm over the one with the blistering red dots and looked away.

After Mama got us back, she said she would never

leave again, but she did, and here we are, running away. Even though I'm ten now, it still hurts that she lied.

"Feet hurt," Anna grumbles, bringing my thoughts back to the dark street, the cold, and how I need to keep my head on straight. As Daddy would say, "Can't see forward if you're lookin' back."

"We're almost there," I assure her, trying not to think about my own achy legs and feet, hoping that Ben and Rachel are home. *What if they aren't? Where will we go?*

While we walk, I try to think of a "plan B," as Daddy calls it. It's the plan you follow when the first one falls through.

CHAPTER 4

BEN AND RACHEL SILVERMAN ARE FOSTER GRAND-parents who take in kids for short periods of time. But to me and Anna, they are more than that. They are the grand-parents we never had. Daddy said our real grandparents lived far away, and it was too expensive for them to come and visit us. We've stayed with the Silvermans a lot over the past two years—sometimes for weeks at a time.

By the time we reach their house, our feet are bleed-ing, our nightshirts are torn, and we're both streaked with dirt. I knock on the door, wondering if any kids are already staying with them. It's okay if they are. I have a plan B. We'll run away again, only this time *back* to our old house. No one would think to look for us there. And even if they locked it all up, I have a way to get in—a secret way that nobody knows about. Not even Anna.

Ben opens the door, takes one look at us, and gasps. He pulls us into a hug, not even minding about the stickers that are poking into his arms. He smells like toothpaste and shaving cream. We smell like dirt and scared stuff, all rolled into one.

"Girls! What happened? What are you doing here in your nightclothes and no shoes?"

"Run away," Anna blurts, clutching her doll and dropping her chin to her chest.

As he ushers us in, the phone rings. We all jump. When Ben answers it, I can tell by his face and voice that it's Mrs. Craig.

"Yes, they're both here. No, they're fine. Yes, yes. Of course we will. Tomorrow?" He looks at us. We both shake our heads as hard as they will shake.

"How about a couple of days?"

I hold my breath. Will they let us stay?

"Okay. We'll wait to hear from you." He hangs up the phone and turns to us. "When she sees you and hears what you have done, Rachel will put extra marks on your charts!"

"Ben is right!" a voice says. Rachel Silverman shuffles sleepily into the room and smothers us with hugs. Her accent is heavy. "Look at you two! For this you get maybe two marks on your charts. Yes, maybe even more. Now you have to earn three stars to get the marks off."

The charts she is talking about are kept on the refrigerator with spaces for stars and marks. For every three stars earned for good behavior, we get one mark removed. For every three marks against us for not being so good, we lose a star.

If we earn five stars and no marks, we get to pick out a treat at the ninety-nine-cent store. If we get all marks and no stars, we have to visit Ms. Thistleberry, the Silvermans' neighbor, who is as prickly as her name.

It's not so bad, really, going to Ms. Thistleberry's. We listen to her complain about every creaky joint she has for two whole hours while peeling vegetables. I like peeling vegetables. I don't tell Rachel, but it's kind of fun to hear about all of Ms. Thistleberry's new creaky spots.

Ms. Thistleberry lives by herself and makes vegetable soups, which people in the neighborhood buy in bucketfuls. Anna and I have peeled a lot of vegetables for Ms. Thistleberry's soups.

"Come," Rachel says, taking our hands. "Let's get some hot cocoa into you and clean you up. A mud bath you will make in my tub." Even though she sounds like she's mad, I know she's as happy to see us as we are to see her.

I look across the hardwood floor toward the kitchen and smile. Ben is already heating up the cocoa. I can see him because the wall between the kitchen and dining room is solid cupboards that open on both sides, and the doors are glass on both sides too, like windows.

A fat pot-bellied stove sits to one side. The crackling fire heats both rooms. As we shuffle toward the kitchen, I look around at the furniture. Ben made it all. He's good with his hands. He also put wood around all the windows. Ben's windows shut tight. No wind gets through them!

The walls have pictures, not of people, but of mountains, meadows, and the ocean. They're so real, it feels like I can step into them and be there, wherever "there" is. The other thing the Silvermans have is a bowl of fish. I bend down and stare, wondering what we must look like to them.

What strange animals they have in this zoo! I picture the orange one saying to the blue. *What are they called again?*

And the blue one would put a fin on his chin and think hard. "Humans," he would say, and bubbles would blub up to the surface. Only underwater it would sound like "Who-moos," which is what we'd be called if fish named us.

Ben already has cocoa set at our places at the table. I take one sip, and the warm chocolate covers my tongue and slides all the way down my throat. Warm cocoa is what safe tastes like.

"Sing a song," Anna murmurs. We've taken a bath, put on the soft flannel nightgowns Rachel saved for us, and been tucked snug in bed. I bury my nose in the sleeve of my nightgown and breathe in the sweet scent of flowers. That's what Rachel's soap smells like: flowers. The bed is big, with a post at each corner—not just a mattress on the floor, like at our real house.

A few months ago, when we last stayed with the Silvermans, Anna and I slept under the bed so scary things had no room to hide. Rachel screamed when she came into the room and found us gone. She thought we had run away again.

When we slid out from under the bed, she said,

"What under the bed are you doing?" Her sentences get more mixed up when she raises her voice.

When I told her how scared we were, she had Ben put a little light under the bed, and we all slept better.

"Sing a song," Anna pleads again. I open my eyes and look at the shadowy face leaning close. Her breath smells like Ben's toothpaste.

"A song?" My voice tries to whisper. She's so close, I feel her nod.

"Daddy's song."

"Why? Are you worried about having another nightmare?"

Anna nods again, planting her hand over the spots on her arm. I rub my eyes and sit up. Too bad Daddy isn't here to sing it himself. I swallow back the hurt. Thoughts of him and Mama turn over and over in my head. *When will you be out of jail? When will the judge let us go home? Where are you, Mama? When will you come home?* I flick on a small flashlight that Ben saved for me.

"Sing!" Anna insists.

I hold back. I know the song she wants. Daddy wrote it just for me—or so he said when he sang it to me on my last birthday. And even though I heard him tell Mama he had written it for her, and then told Anna the same thing when he sang it to her on her birthday months later, it didn't matter. What mattered was that he wrote it and that I knew the whole song by heart.

It's not that I don't like to sing. I do. Singing is my most favorite thing in the world. Daddy says I sing like a songbird—that when I grow up, we'll sing together, him and me. But I also know that singing a song this late might wake up the Silvermans. We'd already woken them up once. I didn't want to push our luck.

"Please?"

"Okay. But I'll have to sing soft, so listen up." I snuggle close to Anna and take a deep breath. But just as I'm about to start, a noise stops me.

"Quick! Under the covers! Somebody's coming!"

What if Mrs. Craig changed her mind and came back to get us? Or worse, the police come and take us away? I flick off the flashlight and cram it under the sheet. Anna starts to tremble. Sometimes being scared makes me breathe so fast, I feel floaty in my head. Other times, it can take the wind right out of me till I think I can't breathe.

I'm not sure which noises are good ones and which are bad ones in the Silvermans' house. The Silvermans are old. They probably wouldn't even hear a burglar sneaking around.

"Pretend to be asleep," I say in a muffled whisper. Under the covers I must sound like fish talking underwater.

"I can't," Anna squeaks. "Scared."

"You can, Anna. Just do like we did when Mama and Daddy were fighting. Close your eyes until the scary stuff goes away." It's the same thing I've told her maybe a hundred times before. Too bad we couldn't close our ears, too.

"Still scared." Anna rolls up into a ball and clutches her doll.

"Shhhh," I whisper back, trying not to sound mean. "Close your eyes and don't open them, no matter what. Okay?" I can feel Anna's head nodding against the pillow.

I pull my head out and wait. My eyes are squeezed so tight, I can see white stars. A flood of light suddenly turns the stars dark, putting a new scary thought into my head—someone is in our room! My heart pounds so hard, I can hear each beat against my pillow. I try to breathe slow and easy, pretending to be asleep, but my breath comes out fast.

"My two sleeping beauties," a woman's voice whispers. I relax. It's only Rachel, checking to make sure that we are still in the room.

I crack one eye open to check on Anna. She's slid out from under the covers but still has a white-knuckled grip on Abby. The doll's eyes are wide open. They are supposed to close when she's laid flat, but sometimes they get stuck. One time one eye stuck open and the other stuck closed—just like when Anna came home from school once and couldn't open a swollen eye; we ran to the neighbor's house. The lady there put ice on it to make the swelling go down and asked a million questions. Anna never did tell anyone how her eye got so puffed up and dark.

Rachel leans closer. She smells of garlic and onions, probably because she has a string of them draped around her neck. "It keeps away the germs," she told me the last time we stayed here. I believed it too. That smell would keep anything away! My nose twitches, and for an awful moment I feel a sneeze coming on. I breathe through my mouth to chase away the feeling.

35

Mrs. Silverman finally seems convinced we're asleep, and leaves. As she shuffles down the hallway, her pajamas make a soft *shoosh, shoosh, shoosh.*

I wait for a moment, listening to the shuffling get softer and softer. "You can open your eyes now. She's gone," I tell Anna, flicking on the flashlight. I aim it at my sister's pale face.

"How do you know she's not hiding outside?" Anna whispers back in a rare full sentence.

I point to the thin streak of dim light under the door. "No feet."

Anna sits up and lets out a long sigh.

"We'd better go to sleep." I settle back onto the bed. "Remember what Mrs. Craig said. We might be going to that new foster home soon. Until Daddy gets out of—" I stop, not wanting to say the *J* word to Anna. All at once I realize why Mrs. Craig calls jail "the special place": to protect Anna from knowing her daddy's locked up in a cage—something that would give her worse nightmares than she already has.

"How come so many places?"

"You mean how come we have to go to so many foster homes?"

Anna nods.

I think about it for a minute. I want to tell her that if she'd quit wetting the bed and biting everyone, we might stand a better chance of staying in just one home instead of bouncing around, but that would hurt her feelings.

"How come?" she repeats.

Anna thinks in pictures, so I know I have to think of images she can see in her head. "Well, foster parents are kind of like spare tires," I say, looking in her eyes for a sign of understanding. "Remember when Daddy had to put the spare tire on his truck because one in front went flat?"

Anna nods.

"Well, foster parents are like spare tires until we get our real tires back, Daddy or Mama. Or until we get a new set of tires," I add. Just saying it gets me wondering what it would be like to get adopted. Not that that will ever happen. We have Daddy and all, but still, what would it be like to have parents who are there all the time and who don't keep disappearing?

Then I start thinking about Daddy locked up in some jail and how much he needs us and how hard he has tried to be good each time he got out and got us back, and suddenly I feel awful for even thinking about what having new parents would be like. He needs me to protect Anna while he and Mama are gone. I push the other thoughts away.

Anna pulls Abby out from under the covers and holds the doll in front of her. "Looks like Mama," she coos.

I look at the doll and back at Anna. "Kind of," I say, even though I really don't think so. Still, I know Anna wants the doll to look like Mama. "Only Mama's arms aren't on backward."

Anna looks puzzled.

"Abby." I point to the doll. "You've got her arms on backward. Want me to fix them?"

Anna started pulling Abby's limbs off after she had to stay at that temporary foster home without me. Anna nods and hands me the doll. About the only time she'll ever let Abby go is to have her put back together. I pull the plastic arms out of their sockets and snap them back into place like I've done a million times before.

"All better," I say, handing Abby back.

"Bad doll! Bad, bad doll." Anna takes Abby and slams her hard against the covers.

I grab her arm. "You're going to break her for good if you keep doing that," I warn. "One of these times, I won't be able to put her back together."

In the shadows, Anna's face crinkles at the thought, which is what her voice sounds like—all crinkled— when she says, "Daddy's song?"

I'd forgotten all about her wanting a song, but not Anna. She remembers everything—good and bad. The more bad that happens, the quieter she gets.

"Okay, okay. I'll sing. But then we have to get some sleep." I clear my throat and in my softest voice sing Daddy's song:

Old tears, they keep falling—
They keep falling for you.
I once held you close to me,
Now you're gone.
But I still see your smile.
I still feel your touch.
I want you to know
I still love you so much.
Old tears, they keep falling,
Falling for you, now you're gone.

As I sing, I picture Daddy up onstage, tall as a giant, gazing down at all the dancing people. A big black cowboy hat shades his sparkling blue eyes from the spotlights. Beads of sweat roll down his forehead and the sides of his face. He raises his arm up and dabs off the sweat with his sleeve, and everyone hoots and cheers. Smiling, he touches the tip of his hat to say thank you.

But mostly I see myself, right there onstage beside him, looking up into his proud, sweaty face, singing his song with all my heart. I reach out and take Daddy's big hand and kiss it. Just thinking about it, I can almost smell the smoke on his fingers.

When I finish the song, I don't even try to stop the hot tears that stream down my cheeks onto the pillow. I look over at Anna, thinking my sister'd be crying now too. But her eyes are closed, and her slow, deep breathing tells me she's already sound asleep.

I pull Mama's letter out from under my pillow, where I hid it, and run my fingers lightly over her words, trying once again to sound them out, picking out the ones I can read.

My dear Sara and Anna,
Ruh-n-eeng. Running.

I stop reading. My thoughts run away with her words. Running what? Out of time? Out of space? Or did she mean running away from me? The girl who is just like Daddy? I look at her picture, trying to see if an answer is maybe hidden in it somewhere. My throat tightens around all the words I can't say to her, and I stuff the letter and picture back under my pillow.

With a snap, I turn off the flashlight.

CHAPTER 5

I OPEN MY EYES TO THE TOUCH OF SUNLIGHT warming my cheeks. Everything feels cozy and safe. Dewdrops shimmer on the window and roll down the glass, reminding me how fast things can change.

I sit up slowly, wondering if Anna's had an accident again. She doesn't mean to wet the bed. It just happens.

"Call the plumber! We've got a leak!" I whisper whenever the sheets are damp. It's something Ben would say. I keep hoping she'll laugh about it, but Anna hardly ever laughs about anything. She's too scared of what might happen if somebody finds the soiled sheets. Every family's reaction is different.

One family rubbed Anna's nose in it. "Bad girl! Bad,

bad girl!" they shouted, like she was a dog or something. Just thinking about it makes me wince. What if those scars on her arm are there because she wet the bed and someone else lost control? Did they grab her and dig their fingernails into her arm? I push away those awful thoughts and shake Anna's thin, bony shoulders, urging her to open her eyes.

"It's morning, Anna. Wake up."

"Caseworker here?" Anna's voice is all froggy. She stretches and rubs her eyes.

"No. We get to stay here a couple of days, remember? Rachel's talking to someone downstairs, but it doesn't sound like Mrs. Craig."

"Like us?"

I study my sister's worried face. Sometimes it's hard to know what she's talking about. "Will the new family like us?" I ask to see if that's what she means. She nods. I smile, secretly pleased that I guessed right.

"Sure, they'll like us. What's not to like?" It's the same thing I told her the last time we were about to be placed in temporary foster care, and the time before that.

"Do you have to go—you know—?"

She turns away and shakes her head.

"Well, I do. Be right back." If I don't get to the bathroom soon, I might be the one having an accident. I slide from the warm sheets and head down the hall toward the bathroom, but I hesitate at the top of the stairs.

The sound of Rachel's soft voice draws me a few steps down, and I peek through the railing. Rachel is sitting in the front room, talking on the phone and drinking coffee. I close my eyes, breathing deep. The smell is comforting. Closing my eyes, for some reason, also helps me hear better, and I strain to make out her words. She has a lazy way of talking. Sometimes her words don't end up in the right order. "Put on the table the napkins," she might say. It's fun to hear her get things mixed up.

Ben says it's because she says the sentence in her head in Russian and then translates it into English, so sometimes the translation comes out funny. Rachel once told me that even after sixty years in this country, she still dreams in Russian!

"I hear welfare kept the family afloat for years, but with the papa making so little money, and with the mama running off—" Rachel leaves the thought hanging, as if the sentence doesn't need an ending. "Kids raising kids," she murmurs. "The courts came finally in and said living like this was unfit. None of the relatives would take them, so the courts did."

When I get that she's talking about us, my chest tightens. Even though I have to pee so bad it hurts, I glue myself to the stairs, wanting to hear more.

"Last I heard, the courts are thinking of charging the mama and papa with neglect."

Neglect? What does that mean? Does that mean that Daddy will have to stay in jail longer? And what about Mama? What are they going to do to her?

"The mama is from the law hiding in Utah or some-place."

Mama is hiding? Is that why she hasn't come to see us? Where is this Utah? How come she has to hide? Why can't we hide with her?

Rachel's voice rises to a harsh whisper. "And a single papa the father is trying to be, but he's got an on-again-off-again nighttime music job that takes him all over. A drummer, he is, though some sense into him someone should drum, leaving those girls alone like that!" Her face turns pink. "A drinking problem he has too!" She leans forward and sets her coffee mug down. "I think somewhere inside he loves those girls." She pats her heart. "Always, always he tries to get them back."

My chest suddenly feels like something heavy is pushing against it. Why is everything such a mess? Why can't someone, anyone, fix it and make it all better?

Rachel nods her head in silent understanding of what the person she's talking to is saying. My guess is that she's talking to Ms. Thistleberry, who's probably peeling vegetables while they talk.

"More money goes into kenneling a pet than the state spends on children in their care! I know. I know. Terrible," Rachel adds, making a clucking noise with her tongue.

I shift uncomfortably. The stair I'm sitting on creaks, and for one awful moment I worry that she's heard me, but she doesn't look up.

Mama is running from the law. Daddy is in jail. Now the court owns us. How will Daddy find us? How will we ever get home?

"It is sad, yes. And you're right. It's hard for older kids like these girls to get adopted." Rachel gathers herself up from the chair. "Everyone wants the little ones. And poor Anna. Around her sister, she does fine, but separate them, and oh my."

The cup in Rachel's other hand rattles against the saucer. She sets it down beside the phone base. "She gets lost somewhere inside here," she says, tapping her head. "And that biting. Poor thing. Chances are . . ."

As she shuffles toward the kitchen, her words grow harder and harder to hear. I lean forward until I'm about to fall. *Chances are what?*

"Even sadder still," she says, returning to the front room, "these poor girls will maybe never see their mama and papa again."

Never see them again? What is she talking about?

I slide from my hiding place and hobble to the bathroom. My stomach hurts so bad. Don't know if it's because I have to go or because of Rachel's words. Maybe both.

Never see Mama and Daddy again? I try to hide the feelings from my face so Anna won't see, but feelings like that are hard to hide.

When I get back from the bathroom, Anna takes one look at my face and her eyes open wider. She sits crouched on the edge of the bed, like a frightened cat preparing to pounce or hiss if anyone comes near.

"Bad?"

"Not really," I lie.

"Nobody wants Anna?"

I catch my breath. Could she have overheard Rachel saying how hard it is for older kids to get adopted?

"No!" I punch a pillow. "We go together, or we don't go at all. Mrs. Craig said so. Remember?"

"Words break," Anna reminds me as she swings her legs down over the side of the bed.

Will Mama's words break? I wonder, slipping her letter and picture out from under the pillow and back into my jacket.

"Hey, watch out for Abby! You almost kicked her in the head." I lean down and scoop up her doll and all its pieces. One by one, I snap them back together. Daddy bought the doll at the flea market for only twenty-five cents and gave it to Anna on her tenth birthday. Mama was long gone, and Daddy even stayed home that day and played with us. It should have been the best birthday ever, but then he went out drinking and got arrested. The judge said he could get us back if he went to parenting classes, so he did.

48

But every time he tried to make things right, something went wrong. Something always goes wrong.

"Maybe some words break, Anna, but not mine." I watch all the worry lines in her forehead soften. "This is one promise that won't ever get broken."

Saying it makes me feel better. Anna is as worried about us getting split up as I am. Every day we wonder who's going to pull us apart. The police? Mrs. Craig? The judge? Foster parents? Who? Who should we be scared of most?

I plop down on the bed and hug Anna. "We go together like the big hand and little hand on a clock," I say.

I get up and fish around in the pocket of my jacket for some buttons Mama left behind. Sometimes in the middle of the night we'd play a game called Tiddlywinks with the buttons. We'd press a big button onto the edge of a smaller one and make it "hop, hop, hop," as Anna would say, until it landed in the cap of Daddy's beer bottle.

But there's another game we play with buttons. I string two of them together onto an old shoelace we found, just like Mama showed me. I tie the lace into a loop and, gripping each end, twirl it round and round until it squeezes my fingers purple. Then I pull the string loose and tight, loose and tight. *Whir, whir, whir.* The two buttons spin so close together that they look like one. Anna might be twelve, but she still likes the button game. I spin the buttons and she calms down, as if pulling the strings draws the fret out of her.

A car door close by slams shut, and Anna and I look to the window.

"Court lady?"

I run to look and see the neighbor lady pulling her car out of her driveway.

"No." I relax a little. "It's just Ms. Thistleberry backing out of her driveway."

When I sit back down on the bed, Cowwy falls to the floor. I bend down and pick him up.

The first thing I notice is that he's damp. I frown, wondering what he might have fallen into. But the smell says it all.

"No!" Anna jumps out of bed and rips the sheets off, wadding them up.

I drop Cowwy and grab the sheets from her.

"Shhhh. It's all right, Anna. I'll say I did it."

"No! No! No! No!" She pulls away and claws at the bed.

I look around for a good hiding place. Maybe I could

drop the sheets out the window and bury them some-where later.

"Don't look," I blurt.

"Where?" She looks around.

"Where I hide the sheets. That's where. That way if Rachel asks where they are, you can say you don't know, and you won't be lying. Hurry, Anna! Hide your eyes."

She presses her shaky hands over her eyes, but I can still see her flushed face behind them.

I quickly rip a pillow from the pillowcase and stuff the soiled sheet inside. Then I drop the pillow onto the floor and kick it under the bed. I can hear Rachel com-ing up the stairs to check on us.

"Crawl under the blanket!" I jump into bed beside Anna right as Rachel knocks on the door. When she opens it, a lone ball of fuzz that must have fallen out of Cowwy rolls across the hardwood floor.

"Rise and shine," she sings out. "Today's your lucky day, and I don't want that anything should spoil it." She swooshes to the closet.

What does she mean, today is our lucky day? I start to feel uneasy but lie stiff, afraid to move for fear she'll notice the missing sheets.

"Look here at what I saved for you. Anna, how about you wear this green cotton dress with on it all the flowers? It goes with your red hair. And the pretty sandals. And Sara, I—"

She stops midsentence, looks at us, and sniffs the air. Her nose wrinkles up and twitches like a rabbit's. She sniffs two more times. "What is this I am smelling?" She says it "smellink." "Anna, did you wet again the bed?"

"No." I can feel Anna's legs shaking under the cover. I reach over and squeeze her hand. She squeezes back.

"You wouldn't be telling to me a little story now, would you?" Rachel says, patting the blanket. "You know we can get those special pants for Anna for nighttime."

Anna makes a face. "Baby pants."

"They're not baby pants, Anna," Mrs. Silverman says, bending down to look under the bed.

My heart thumps so hard it feels like it's going to beat right out of me. *Think fast! Hurry! She'll figure it out!* And if she tells Mrs. Craig, we might not get into a good foster home. No one wants a bed-wetter. I grip my end of the blanket and hold tight.

"She's here!" I shout.

CHAPTER 6

"WHAT ON EARTH? WHO'S HERE?" RACHEL SHUFFLES toward the door.

"Mrs. Craig! She's here!" I slide out from under the blanket and jump up and down on the bed—something I know Mrs. Silverman never allows.

"Stop that jumping right this instant or a mark I'll give you on the chart!" she scolds, wagging a finger. With heavy steps, she crosses the room and bends, peering out the window. I sneak Anna a grin and wink, just like Daddy used to wink at me when he was playing a trick on Mama.

"She was not to be here until tomorrow. Her car I do not see." Rachel stops talking and slowly turns around. "If this is a clever trick you're playing because your sister wet again the bed, then you, missy, are in big trouble. You'll make two marks on the chart. Maybe even lose a star. You know better than to tell stories or hide things. I don't harm your sister. She has accident, we wash. Now put on yourself some clothes and come down when for breakfast you are ready. And bring the dirty sheets with you."

When she leaves, Anna's eyes widen. "Soup lady?"

She crawls out of bed, and I laugh.

"Worker here tomorrow?"

I pull the dress Rachel has picked out for me over my head and help Anna with hers, then nod.

For both of us, tomorrow will come too soon.

"Look good?" Anna twirls and models her dress. I study my sister from the top of her head to the clear plastic sandals on her feet. The shiny gold half-heart necklace that hangs around her neck matches the half heart I wear around mine.

It was a present from Mama. *Never take it off,* she said. *Look after each other. You're sisters. Sisters stick together.* We didn't know she'd be gone the next day. I'm wondering if she did.

"Look good?" Anna repeats a little impatiently. She stops twirling and puts her hands on her hips.

"All I can say is, with all those flowers on that dress, you better hope there aren't any bees out there." That got a smile. But Anna's smiles never last long, and this one is gone almost as fast as it came.

"You look like Mama," I add. She does look like Mama, I think. Same burnt-red hair. Same sad, faraway look in her sea-green eyes. But that is about all I can remember of Mama. Not a day goes by that we don't study the face of every stranger, looking for some sign of her. Will we know her if she walks by?

It's been so long now since I've seen her that the memory of her face is starting to fade. I know Anna misses her so bad that it probably hurts to look in a mirror and be reminded over and over of who we lost.

"You look like Daddy." Anna gives each word equal weight. Another small smile comes and goes.

I raise my eyebrows. "You think so?" I brush back my long bangs with fanned fingers and look hard at the face in the mirror. I count ten new freckles that I haven't seen before. They must have been hiding under the dirt that washed off in last night's bath. The hot water felt so good. Even the toothbrush on my teeth felt good.

Rachel saved our toothbrushes from the last time we stayed, like she knew we'd be back.

"I do have his nose." I lean close for a better look. "And his blue eyes, maybe. But other than that, I don't think I look like him." *When I look at you, I see him.* Mama's words still ring in my ears.

"Or smell," Anna adds, pinching her nose. I know she's talking about how Daddy smells after he's been drinking. And the smoke that settles in his hair and on his clothes and breath. Much as I got scared when he thundered home smelling mean, I miss the smell now. At least he came with it.

"Don't want to go."

I don't answer. Instead, when we finish dressing, I drop the soiled sheets into the washer downstairs and lead the way into the kitchen for breakfast. Rachel is humming as she cooks. It's as if she forgot all about the sheets. I love that about old people. They can forget things that need to be forgotten.

Down the hall, Ben is hammering at something. I can't see him, but I know that if there's a hammer or a wrench nearby, he's close, if not attached to it.

And just as if my thoughts led him, he steps into

56

the kitchen. "My two favorite girls!" His eyes sparkle. Funny about smiles, how one always seems connected to another. It's that way with Ben, anyway. His smiles always make me smile.

He sets his hammer on the table and stretches out his arms. First Anna gets a big bear hug, then me. His hearing aid makes a high beeping noise with each squeeze.

"Mm-mm, mmm, *mm!*" he says, like we are a bowl of Ms. Thistleberry's soup. "Did I tell you yet how good it is to see you both again?"

"You just told us last night!" I remind him.

"Was that you under all that dirt? And here I thought it was some other little girl I hadn't met yet."

I laugh. He's so funny. And he talks with a thick accent, like Rachel, only his voice is grumblier and he doesn't mix up his words as much.

"You will join me for breakfast?" The light in his eyes dances as he settles into a chair and scoots up to the table. The legs of the chair make little burp noises when they scrape against the floor.

To answer, I sit beside him, where Rachel has already set a place for me. Anna sits across from him, smiling shyly.

"What are you fixing?" I ask him.

"The tub. The drain, it doesn't drain so good. So I fix. There isn't much in life that can't be fixed. You just have to have the right tools." He picks up a hammer beside his plate and sets it down gingerly, as if it's the one tool needed most in life.

"After breakfast, you will maybe help me fix the plug in the tub?"

I smile and nod at the same time. Ben always has fun things to do, and he always let me take out a screw with his screwdriver, or hammer in a nail.

He can't stand up straight anymore. He says old age is weighing him down. His hair is old and gray. His teeth are old, too. But his raisin-brown eyes, flecked with gold, sparkle under a fluff of bushy gray eyebrows.

Every now and then a stormy look blows over Ben— usually after he's listened to the news on the radio—but for the most part, he's a gentle, quiet old man who can fix just about anything. Except our family.

Rachel plops a plate of steaming French toast sprinkled with cinnamon and smothered in maple syrup at my place.

"Put on your lap your napkin," she reminds us.

I take tiny bites of French toast and chew each one slowly, letting the maple syrup get all over my tongue. I want the flavor to last as long as possible. When I finish the last of the toast, I pick up my plate and lick off some syrup.

"Ah, *kia!*" Rachel cries, throwing her hand to her chest. "Sara! What are you doing?"

She says the word "doing" like it ends with a *k,* and swooshes over to reach for my plate. "You are not a cat drinking milk, yes? We don't lick plates."

"But it gets all the syrup off," I grumble, not wanting to give up the dish just yet.

"Yes, but it is not doink the polite think," she answers, putting the plate in the sink and running hot water over it.

Following my plate to the sink, I lean over and watch the hot water lick the last of the syrup away. "Polite to who? The plate?" I ask.

Ben laughs and answers, "To the plate. To the people around you at the table. To—"

"And you!" Rachel scolds, reaching for his hammer. "This does not on the breakfast table go."

Ben raises his bushy eyebrows and pouts. "First she

takes my hammer," he says. "What next? My hands to hammer with? My arms to hold my hands with? My—"

"Enough is enough!" Rachel throws her hands over her head, shooing all of us from the table after we've finished our meal. "Hands to hammer with! I'll show you hands to hammer with!"

I grin at Anna. Too bad all people can't argue like this. No hitting. No throwing things. Just playful words bouncing back and forth.

CHAPTER 7

ALL MORNING I HELP BEN FIX THINGS, HANG
pictures, and move furniture. Rachel likes to redecorate.

"It gives a new look to the place!" she says, pointing
to where a chair should go.

"And a new something to trip over," Ben grumbles,
moving it. Anna and I look at each other and grin. While
I help Ben, Anna helps Rachel bake.

"Are those cookies done yet?" Ben hollers. I know
the smell is driving him crazy. Me, too.

"Not yet! Hold on your horses!"

We barely finish moving things and snacking on
cookies when the doorbell rings. I instantly recognize Mrs. Craig's voice. She waltzes into the kitchen,

bringing with her a scent of flowery perfume. "Look at how pretty you two look! All scrubbed and clean." She gives us both a quick, scolding look, then checks her watch. "I think you know that what you did last night was not right. Thank goodness you're both safe.

"There's been a change of plans. I know you had hoped to stay longer with the Silvermans, but some other children are scheduled to stay here for a couple of days."

I stare at the floor, listening to the drip of the kitchen faucet. My feet are puffy and still hurt from the scratches. After a long, empty silence, I look up.

"Are you all ready for your new adventure?" Mrs. Craig asks, glancing out the window like she's afraid her car might drive off without her.

I look sideways at Anna. How, I wonder, do other kids get ready for these "new adventures," as Mrs. Craig calls them? Sleeping in strange houses with strange people who call us clever names like "pumpkin"—something Anna always got stuck with because of her red hair— "peaches," or any number of other food names. Never knowing if we are staying, moving to another placement, or finally going home.

Mrs. Craig smiles hurriedly at the Silvermans and not at us. "Cheer up, now. There's a nice family that's taking you in, and I want to take you over to meet them."

I stare out the window at leaves swirling together on the grass. Not that long ago, Anna and I had played like that, twirling around. Then everything started twisting out of control.

Mrs. Craig hooks an arm around Anna's shoulder. I look at Anna, hoping she won't spit at her or bite her, which is something she does when grown-ups get too close, but it doesn't look like Anna is even paying attention. Instead, she pulls out of Mrs. Craig's grasp and curls up in a chair, hugging her knees, like she's trying to hold herself together. At least this time she's on the chair instead of under it. I know what she's feeling. I want to crawl under something and hide.

Anna looks up suddenly, as if coming back from some lost thought. She senses things, like when someone or something is approaching. A giant cloud-shadow covers the house, turning it suddenly dark—so dark, the light-sensitive kitchen lights flick on, then off, and then on again.

It can only mean something bad is going to happen.

63

Saying good-bye to Ben and Rachel is always hard. I try not to hold on too tight to them or to anyone. It hurts too much to let go. I stare out the window at the clouds that have turned the whole city dark.

Two seconds after we climb into Mrs. Craig's station wagon, the sky splits open, dumping water by the bucket-load onto the car, the street, the houses. Everything.

Huge raindrops smack against the windshield, drowning out the soft popping sounds of Anna pulling the arms and legs off of Abby.

"We're in for a wet one," Mrs. Craig says, fastening her seat belt. She looks past a stack of forms and papers strewn on the passenger side and cranks her neck around to check that Anna and I have fastened our seat belts. Parts of Anna's doll are all over the seat. Mrs. Craig frowns slightly, turns back, and starts the engine.

Anna's face is as wet as the sky. I can't look at her for fear that I'll start crying too. Instead I stare at the trees, wind whipping through them. Rain drums hard against the top of the car, making it too loud for anyone to talk—almost too loud to even think, which is fine with me. I don't feel like thinking.

All I want to do is sleep, then wake up and find out this

SARA LOST AND FOUND

is all a bad dream and we are on our way to our real house, where Daddy, or maybe even Mama, is waiting for us.

The drive is long and slow. Water shoots up in fan-like sprays on either side of the car, like the parting of a great sea. And then it's over. Flash floods are like that. Clouds burst open so suddenly that there's no time to think. Then, *poof!* Just like that, they're gone.

"You'll like the MacMillans," Mrs. Craig says, peering up at the sky like she's talking to the clouds. "They're good people. The dad, Dan, is a doctor. Barbara, his wife, is a teacher. She teaches nurses how to nurse," she adds.

I glance over at a plastic arm lying on the seat, thinking that Anna's doll could sure use a nurse.

"They're really looking forward to having you stay with them," Mrs. Craig adds, turning a corner.

I know we should say something like, "That's nice," or "We are too," but we don't. We just sit there. Nothing we say changes things. I finger the necklace Mama gave me. *Look after your sister.* Her words slip like a leash around my neck.

By the time we reach the new people's house, the rain has nearly stopped. Still, water gushes down the gutter like a raging river.

I stare at it, awed by how strong it is. Everything in its path is carried away, no matter how little or big. A red rubber ball floats past, along with garbage cans with no lids and leaves ripped from the trees. If we had a boat, Anna and I would float as far as the water would take us.

"Now, remember. This is just a temporary stop until I can find you girls a more permanent home. Be careful getting out. I don't want the water to knock you down. What a mess."

I scramble out of the car onto the driveway, then off the curb into the gutter. The strong current rushes over my shoes, soaking my feet. It's wonderfully cold and sends an exciting chill through me.

"Anna! Sara! Come away from there! What are you doing? Girls!"

In the rush of water, I can barely hear Mrs. Craig's voice. The cold liquid feels good on my sore, hot feet. A movement, not like water gushing, catches my eye. Two houses up the street, something—an animal, maybe— is struggling to hold on to the curb.

What is it? A rat? I think about Hope buried back home. *No, too big.*

I try to walk toward whatever it is for a closer look, but the water fights to hold me back. When I try to lift my feet, it feels like I have iron shoes on. Suddenly, the animal loses its grip and is torn from the curb.

"A kitten!" I shout over my shoulder to Anna, who is right behind me. I watch the kitten struggle to stay alive. When I try to walk toward it, the water pushes me back, just like Anna pushes people away with all her biting and spitting. I'm sure this kitty didn't know how powerful a storm could be before she got swept up in it.

She does now.

"Leave it, Sara!" Mrs. Craig shouts from the porch. She has started down the sidewalk toward us. "The water's too fast. Come over here where it's safe!"

Leave it? I watch the tiny kitten fighting to stay above water. I can't just leave it. The kitten is coming toward me so fast, I know I have to brace myself against the rushing water to try to catch it before it's swept away.

Oh please, please let me catch it. I can see the animal clearly now. I am right. It's a small black-and-white kitten, crying out every time its little head comes above water. *Mew, mew.*

67

"Over here, little fella!" I bend over, stretching my arms. Three, two, one—*thoop!*

The minute the soggy kitten thumps against my legs, I clamp my hands around its soaked little body. I can feel it trembling through my fingers and know that it's shaking from more than just being cold and wet. I look down the road. For a split second, I want to just sit right down with the kitten in that gutter and ride the water wherever it will take me. Instead, I hug the kitten close as Anna and I slosh across the grass and to the door.

We shiver and drip on the front porch while a woman I would guess to be Mrs. MacMillan runs inside for towels.

"Of all the days for a freak storm!" Mrs. MacMillan cries, handing first me, then Anna, a towel. I wrap it around the kitten.

"Oh no, honey. Not around the cat. It'll get hair all over the towel, not to mention fleas. Oh dear. Just wrap it around yourself." Mrs. MacMillan tries to wrap the towel around me as she talks.

"You watch," she says over my head to Mrs. Craig. "In an hour, there won't be a trace of water on the street.

I don't even want to look at the garden out back," she moans. "I just know the storm ruined the pumpkins."

I know her talk is nervous talk. New foster parents are always nervous when we arrive.

"The pumpkins will be fine," a man's voice says. "Are you girls all right?" I peer up at someone who I guess is Dr. MacMillan. He's a tall, tanned man with almost no hair. He has blue eyes like Daddy's, only the skin around his eyes is smooth.

The three grown-ups look at Anna and me dripping. Anna bends over, trying to take off her wet shoes. I grip the cat, shivering.

"Poor things. Let's get you inside." Mrs. MacMillan starts for the door.

"Dad!" A wail comes from upstairs. "The roof is leaking in the bathroom."

Dr. MacMillan shakes his head. "Never a dull moment. I'll look in a minute, Pablo," he calls. "Come meet your new sisters!" He hesitates, looking from the sky to the car and back to us, then adds, "And bring some dry clothes!"

Pablo? What a strange name. Shorts and T-shirts fall onto the floor from somewhere above. I hand the kitten to Mrs. Craig, asking her to please hold it until Anna and I come back from changing.

Mrs. Craig makes a face and dangles the cat away from her. I grin, hoping she won't let the cat go.

Mrs. MacMillan shows us to the downstairs bathroom, where Anna and I change. Anna is soon swallowed up by a large white T-shirt that comes clear down to her knees. The arms stop at the bend in her elbows, hiding those spots. Under the T-shirt, she's put on a pair of yellow shorts.

As for me, I put on a pink T-shirt that has children dancing around a drum, and shorts that are so big and hang so low, they feel like they might fall off.

When we return to the front porch, Mrs. Craig hands me the wet, meowing kitten.

"That's better!" Mrs. MacMillan exclaims, smiling broadly. "Look!" She points to the sky. "The sun! What did I tell you? You watch. The pumpkins will be ruined."

More nervous talk. I decide to make her feel better.

"Nice house," I say.

"Well, now!" Mrs. Craig sings out, smiling approvingly at me. "Let's make this official. Sara, Anna, I'd like you to meet your new temporary foster family, the MacMillans."

I know the script. The next move is mine: Stick out hand. Shake. Say hellos. Look up. Smile a lot. The first face I look up at is Barbara MacMillan's. She's a short, round, friendly-faced woman with shoulder-length brown hair. She has a big smile. When she talks, her words kind of march. Mrs. Craig had said she taught nurses how to nurse. Maybe part of her teaching is giving orders, and that's why she talks like she does.

I am right about the balding guy. It's Dr. Dan MacMillan, her husband.

A boy, brown as a roasted peanut, who looks like he's a little older than me, comes around the doorway and stares at us.

"This is our son—Pablo," Mrs. MacMillan announces, putting her hands on the boy's shoulders and moving him toward us. "His adoption was official four years ago yesterday. We still celebrate every year."

"Hi." Pablo is almost a whole head taller than Anna, which makes him a head and a half taller than me. His eyes are like round black olives, darker than Ben Silverman's, and his smile is quick and white. His dark brown hair is long on top and falls down on his forehead

71

in curly strands. He has on cutoffs, a sun-melt yellow tie-dyed T-shirt, and sandals.

"Where'd that come from?" Pablo points to the lump of wet fur that I'm holding.

I just stare at him. Mrs. Craig steps in. "That's a kitten that Sara saved from the storm."

"Just what this neighborhood needs, another stray," Mrs. MacMillan says, still holding on to Pablo, like if she let go, she'd lose her balance or him. "The block is full of them. Kittens everywhere. Let's all go into the dining room, shall we?" She ushers us in, looking long and hard at the cat as I pass by.

"Keep it?" Anna begs, patting the kitten's head.

"It might be somebody's pet, honey. Or maybe its family is looking for it—we don't know. I think we should just put it outside and let it find its way home."

"Maybe it doesn't have a home," I blurt. *Didn't she just call it a stray?*

Mrs. MacMillan glances over at Mrs. Craig, then smiles at me.

"Well, you're right. I don't know if it has a home or not. The neighborhood is overrun with kittens no different than this one. But it appears you girls have taken a liking to it—" She frets a moment and does a *hem-haw* thing. "Mmm. How about this. You can keep it, but it has to stay outside. And if you could, try to keep it out of my garden."

Outside? I stare at her. *Has she looked around?* What if the storm comes back? The kitten could drown. Or get hit by a car or eaten by a dog. Still, I nod, clinging to the kitten. "Can we dry her off real good before she goes out?"

"Of course. Let me get a rag, though. Don't use the towel."

"We'll sneak her in later," I whisper to Anna as Mrs. MacMillan races off to find a rag.

"Sneaker," Anna agrees. I grin. Anna has just named the cat.

"It looks like things are going to be fine," Mrs. Craig says as we all round the table. "Let's take a moment, before I leave"—she stops to check her watch to be sure she has time for whatever it is we're taking a moment for—"and tell the girls about your upcoming move."

Upcoming move? What move?

Mrs. MacMillan returns with a torn-up towel and hands it to me. Anna and I sit beside each other at the dining room table. I don't make any move to put Sneaker outside, but no one says anything.

"Juice, anyone?" Mrs. MacMillan holds up a pitcher of orange juice.

Anna and I nod.

"It was too noisy in the car to really explain the situation to you girls," Mrs. Craig began, glancing this time at the clock on the wall, "but the MacMillans are moving to South America. Dr. MacMillan is part of a team of surgeons called Doctors Without Borders that goes there every year for six months to help sick children and perform surgeries on those with deformities."

South America? Anna and I are moving to South America? I barely know where that is.

"Isn't that pretty far from here?" I manage to say. *How will Daddy find us?*

The whole room grows the kind of quiet that makes people cough in church. Any good feelings I might have start to slip away.

"Oh, honey. I didn't mean that you and Anna would be moving too. Just the MacMillans."

Like I said before, we're learning not to get too attached to places or people.

"Not us?" Anna hangs her head. I can tell she likes the MacMillans. Except for the Silvermans, this is a first.

"With everything that's going on with your mom and dad, this really wouldn't be the best time to go out of the country. In the meantime," Mrs. Craig adds, standing up like she's readying to go, "the Silvermans said that they might be able to fill in until I find another family who can take you girls—that is, until we hear more about what's happening with your parents. How does that sound?"

Anna glances at me and looks down at the floor again. The news about the Silvermans is good. I look around. The house seems nice enough. It has carpet the color of sand, which feels warm on my feet. The front room has the biggest brown couch I've ever seen. It's like three couches in one. Good thing it's here and not at the Silvermans'. Ben could hurt himself moving a couch like that.

Books are everywhere. Shelves and shelves of them. Some standing. Some with the covers facing out. Some tipped over. I look at them, wishing I could read them. Anna and I love books. Pictures line the walls, like windows to another world, a world of aunts, uncles, cousins, grandparents, friends, birthdays, weddings, and—I stare at Pablo's picture—adoption.

The house is friendly enough, I tell myself. We'd just have to not get too used to it.

The kitchen, meanwhile, smells of Ms. Thistleberry's soup. I wonder if Mrs. MacMillan buys from her too.

"Does that sound okay to you girls? Staying here for a while, then going back to the Silvermans?" Dr. MacMillan asks.

I shrug and nod for both of us. The silence that fills the room suddenly feels like a living, breathing thing, and Anna fidgets.

"Now that that's cleared up, how about a tour of the house? Then we can all have lunch together," Mrs. MacMillan chirps brightly.

"I'll walk you to your car," Dr. MacMillan says, holding the door open for Mrs. Craig. "Unless you'd care to join us."

"I really should be getting along. I have another call to make." Mrs. Craig gives us both a quick hug. "You girls take care, okay? I'll call you early in the week to see how things are going. And Barbara has my number if you need to talk to me."

I nod, not wanting her to go. Not yet. But she leaves. Wishing doesn't always make things happen.

"Do you want to see your room?" Pablo looks from me to Anna.

Anna leans close to my ear. "Hide Sneaker," she whispers as we head for the stairs.

I grin.

"Ah-ah. It's not nice to whisper when others are around," Mrs. MacMillan says behind us. "No keepers of secrets in this house!"

Keepers of secrets. *Ha*. The name fits Anna and me better than any of them know.

That night, after a dinner of mashed potatoes, salad, corn on the cob, and roast beef, I slip a slice of meat into a Baggie I find on the counter and head upstairs. Curled up in bed, I lie awake staring at the millions of stars outside the window, wondering which one's the wishing star. I pick out one that looks promising and wish long and hard that Daddy will come and get us.

Even though she has her own bed to sleep in, Anna crawls in with me. Mrs. MacMillan comes in and lingers near the door.

"Is there anything I can get you girls? Water? A blanket?" she asks.

I shake my head and turn back to the stars. They hold what we want, not her.

As Mrs. MacMillan goes over what we might do the next day, she turns on a fan to cool us. Anna has already fallen asleep. Even the wind outside has settled down.

Not me, though. Not yet. Mrs. MacMillan leans down and kisses the top of my head. When she leaves the room, I slip from under the covers and tiptoe to the closet, where Sneaker is hiding, and give her the meat from dinner. While she eats, I wonder if I should let her out.

Is Mrs. MacMillan right? Does Sneaker have a home? Am I keeping her from a family that's out searching for her, just like Daddy might be searching for us?

I tuck the kitten in bed with us. She licks her whiskers and smells like roast beef. "Tomorrow we'll look for your family," I tell her.

A bright slip of moon smiles through the window. Beside it, a star burns brightly. Closing my eyes, I make one more wish, then fall asleep.

CHAPTER 8

I WAKE THE NEXT MORNING WITH THE SAME question Anna and I always have when we get placed in a new home: What do we call the foster parents? Mom? Dad? Neither feels right. Dr. and Mrs. MacMillan? Yuck. Barbara and Dan? I sigh. Some grown-ups, like Ben and Rachel, don't mind kids calling them by their first names. Others think it's rude. Which would it be here?

Anna's side of the bed is empty. I get up. I hear Pablo coming up the stairs, humming.

"Have you seen Anna?" I ask, following him down the hallway toward his room.

He shakes his head. At his door, he turns around to

face me, bracing his arms against the frame.

"Uh-uh. My room's off-limits. You can only come in when I'm here or when I invite you. I don't want anyone messing with my stuff."

Behind him, I can see Anna messing with his stuff. I doubt he invited her. She turns the strange stump of wood she's holding upside down. A shivering, rolling, rainlike sound drifts through the room.

"Like that," Pablo said, taking the stump from Anna and marching her out into the hall. "What are you doing in here?"

Anna reaches up to grab the stump of wood. When she does, Pablo pulls it away and catches her by the arm. Wrong move. Before I can call out, her teeth find their mark.

"Hey!" Pablo jerks back his hand. A full moon of teeth indents marks his arm, then disappears. "What did you do that for?"

Anna's eyes narrow, and a sort of growl comes out of her. I see Sneaker pawing at the covers on Pablo's bed. It all makes sense to me now. Sneaker got out, Anna went to Pablo's room to get her, saw the noisemaker, and got distracted—

"So, what is that thing that Anna was playing with?" I ask.

Pablo holds up the piece of wood and turns it over to make the soft shivering sound again. "It's a rainmaker from Chile, which is where I come from." He looks back and forth at us, his dark eyes dancing. "Who do you think made all that rain yesterday?"

"Yeah, right." Like he can really make it rain. Still, maybe things happen differently in Chile. Maybe he really can make rain.

"All you need is a magic stick," he answers, tossing the rainmaker onto his bed.

If only it were that easy.

He hesitates a minute, then picks it up and hands it to Anna. "Okay, play with it if you want."

Anna holds it like it's made of glass. The sound of rain seems to calm her.

"So, your real mom and dad. Where are they?" I ask, following him and Anna down the stairs. I feel Sneaker brush against my foot as she dashes past.

"Hey, how'd that cat get inside?" Pablo grabs at Sneaker and misses. When he gets to the bottom of the stairs, he opens the door, and she runs out.

"My birth parents live in Chile, though I've never met them," he answers, closing the door. "I lived in an orphanage there until the MacMillans found me. They're my real mom and dad now. I've lived with them for four years. Dad fixed my lip on one of his trips to Chile. Now no one can tell it was deformed."

I had noticed the tiny scars around Pablo's mouth, but I thought a cat had scratched him.

"They brought me back with them to America," he adds. "I like it here, and I like my American parents."

"Do you ever miss your other mom and dad? You know, your birth parents?" I prod.

We had passed through the family room and were heading for the kitchen. Dr. and Mrs. MacMillan were out on the back porch, drinking coffee.

"Miss them?" He frowns and leans on the counter in the kitchen. "I guess I don't think about it that much. I didn't know them, so what's to miss?"

I look away. What's to miss? How different feelings can be. I'm about to ask Pablo if he ever thought he'd see them again, when I see Anna's and my clothes hanging up to dry in the laundry room. My jacket! Mama's letter! Her picture! What if they were found, or worse, ruined?

"Why? Do you miss yours?" Pablo looks at me, eyebrows raised, waiting for an answer. But all I can think about is my jacket and Mama's letter.

"Yeah," I say in haste. "But maybe it's because I know who they are."

He nods and follows my gaze, then seems to guess my thoughts. "You don't need to be worried about your jacket. Mom sewed the lining."

"She *what*? Did she sew it before or after she washed it?" *Could she have found Mama's letter? Did she read it?*

"I don't know. What difference does it make?"

I rush over and pull my jacket from the hanger. My worst thought comes true. The letter and Mama's picture are gone. I slump on a chair, letting the jacket fall around my legs.

Pablo looks at me, frowning. "You sure are attached to that jacket."

Dr. and Mrs. MacMillan come in from the porch and grin at us. "Well, well! Look who's awake. And hungry, I bet." Mrs. MacMillan ushers us all out to the back porch, where a table is set with fresh fruit and toast for breakfast.

Anna sits down by me and whispers in my ear, "Mama's letter?"

I look away, not wanting to answer, not wanting her to know that Mama's letter and picture are gone. How could I have let the jacket out of my sight?

Anna pulls off Abby's arm and uses the hand as a spoon to scoop up fruit. When the fruit falls off the hand, she spears it and then puts a whole chunk of fruit in her mouth.

The MacMillans watch without saying anything.

Forks clink against plates. Around us, birds chatter and hop from one branch to another. Across the yard, three crows start to argue. A plane lumbers low overhead, drowning them out.

I tilt my head. The sweet fruit juice rolls to the back of my throat and I swallow.

I go for another bite and look over at Dr. Dan's hands. Smooth. Long fingers. So different from Daddy's thick, calloused hands. Behind Dr. Dan, I see three drums against the wall.

Dr. Dan looks to see what I'm looking at and smiles, raising his eyebrows and giving that look people get when they figured something out. He looks back at me. "You play drums?"

I shake my head. "My daddy does, but his drums

84

aren't like those. Daddy uses sticks. He plays guitar, too."

I look over at Anna, who nods.

"Well, the drums we have are called Kungas, or conga drums. They're from Africa. I got them on one of my trips there."

Pablo gets up and sits behind them. "Drums can sound like heartbeats," he says, making a soft thumping beat with his fingertips, "or they can sound like rain." He makes like ants crawling over the top of the drums.

"Or it can sound like thunder," Pablo says, raising his hands up and bringing them down in a wild beat that gets my heart pounding.

"Want to make a rainstorm?" I nod so hard my chin jiggles, but when I look at Anna, she shrinks back like someone's going to hit her.

"Come on, Anna. It'll be fun!" I reach for her hand and pull her up from her chair.

"You sit here," Pablo says to me, patting a stool next to him, "and you, Anna, sit here." He pats the stool on the other side of him.

"Each of us has a different pattern. Don't worry, I'll teach you. They're not hard, so don't freak out, okay?"

We both nod.

"Anna, your pattern goes like his." He pats his right hand twice on his drum, followed by his left hand, which he also pats twice. While he pats, he says her name. "An-na. An-na."

"An-na, An-na," she whispers, tapping her drum. I hold my breath. *She's doing it! She's playing the drum.*

"That's it," Pablo says, nodding for her to keep going. "You are the important beat, Anna. You keep us on track.

"Now you, Sara. Your beat is this." He turns his attention to me and taps on the drum. "On, pause, Wis-con-sin. On, pause, Wis-con-sin."

I try to match his beat, but it's hard with Anna tapping out her beat.

"Keep trying. You almost have it," Pablo urges. "Just say, 'On, pause, Wis-con-sin' over and over while you tap, and when you say 'pause,' don't hit the drum." He plays it along with me to help me pick up the beat.

I finally get it.

"Now I'll add my beat. 'Mis-sis-sip-pi, go. Mis-sis-sip-pi, go.'"

It takes a second, and then something magical

happens. A gentle rainstorm fills the patio. I look over at Anna. Her head is tipped back and her eyes are closed. She has a little smile on her face. It's been a long time since I've seen her looking so normal. So at peace.

When the storm ends, Mrs. MacMillan and Dr. Dan clap wildly. Pablo gives us a high five and we head back to the table feeling all pumped up.

Pablo leans back in his seat, resting his head against the top of it. I lean my head back, but it doesn't even come close to touching the top of the chair.

"We made a good team just then."

Dr. Dan nods. "That's sort of like how I feel about the doctors that I work with. We all bring a different skill to the job at hand and help make a difference in someone's life."

He pauses and glances at me. "You look thoughtful, Sara. What are you thinking about?"

"Animals," I answer, and he leans in toward the table and smiles.

"Any particular ones?" His eyebrows shoot up.

I nod. "The ones that were used to make those drums. Daddy says the top of the drum is called a head, and that the 'skin' on the head is the skin of a cow, and the thick string holding it to the wood is made from pig gut.

"It used to make me sad to hear him play his drums, because I knew animals died to make it, but he said that the spirit of the animal and the tree cut down to make the drum stay with it, and that playing the drum honors them."

Anna nods and looks back at the drums.

"Wow. You gave me something to think about, Sara."

Pablo looks at me and gives me a thumbs-up, like I'd said something major. Or maybe it's hard to come up with something Dr. Dan has to think about. He already sounds like he knows pretty much everything.

"Have you girls had enough to eat?" Mrs. MacMillan offers Anna a fresh green bean from a bowl of beans on the table, but Anna shakes her head.

I nod, but tuck a paper napkin in my pocket in case Anna and I get hungry later.

"Good! Then let's carry these dishes to the kitchen and relax a little. How does that sound?"

I grab my plate and bowl and Anna grabs hers, and we turn to follow Mrs. MacMillan into the house and then to the kitchen.

But before we get there, Anna looks over her shoulder at me and grins. I grin back, but smiles can turn to "Oh no" very fast, which is what my smile does. Anna sees the change. I know because I can see the alarm go off in her eyes.

CHAPTER 9

TOO LATE TO SHOUT A WARNING. TOO LATE TO CATCH the flying plates as Anna trips over a circle rug on the tile floor.

It's funny how a sound can shatter more than a plate. When the dishes hit the tile and explode into a million pieces, something explodes inside of me. The whole world turns slo-mo, and just like that, I'm back at home. Mama's hurling a plate across the kitchen and it smashes against the wall. Spaghetti falls in wet strands to the floor. Mama's yelling, but Anna and I can't hear her. We're screaming too.

Anna yelps, falling hard onto the floor. Her cry startles me. I let go of the bowl and plate I'm holding to reach out for her, when another crash fills my head.

I look in time to see Dr. Dan leap over the rug toward Anna. I catch the shock on Mrs. MacMillan's face. Her hands are in the air like someone's about to shoot her.

Pablo stops short behind me and scoops me up. For a second I am flying toward the ceiling, then just as fast I fall and Pablo catches me. My foot is bleeding.

I look behind Pablo at Anna. Dr. Dan has grabbed her and I open my mouth to shout, but Anna's teeth find their mark and sink into Dr. Dan's hand.

A noise comes out of him, and the house becomes an echo of cries, yelps, and howls.

It's a different kind of sound than our "team" tapping out a rainstorm. I see the look on Anna's face and know she is mortified. Our eyes meet and the feeling passes between us.

I heard at school once that twins do that, have feelings and thoughts pass between them.

Anna and I aren't twins, but we share a different kind of twin: fear.

And the fear-twins don't need to learn a language to understand one another.

When the glass settles and the howling stops,

silence fills the room. All that can be heard is Anna whimpering, "Let go. Let go."

Pablo sets me down gently, but holds my shoulders so I don't bolt across the broken glass toward Anna.

"Don't anybody move," Mrs. MacMillan says, then breaks her own rule and steps into the kitchen, returning with a broom and dustpan. "Dan, how's your hand?"

Dr. Dan takes in a deep breath and lets it out slowly. "She barely broke the skin. It should be okay."

"She didn't mean to bite you," I tell him quietly. "She doesn't like to be touched."

Meanwhile, Anna has cocooned at the end of a couch, wrapping her arms tightly around her knees.

"Pablo, can you carry Sara into the kitchen and put her on a chair so I can check to make sure there's no glass in that cut on her foot?"

"Sure." Pablo swoops me up and lands me on a chair by the kitchen table. He had worn shoes, so he didn't get cut. My feet are bare.

As Mrs. MacMillan sweeps up bits of broken plates and glasses, Pablo rushes to get a trash can. Dr. Dan stays by Anna. I can't see them, but I can picture them sitting across from one another in an awkward silence.

"I know I scared you, Anna, and I am very sorry. I would never hurt you." He pauses. "In the future, I'll try not to scare you, but it would help if you would just say the word 'No' instead of biting.

"You bit my hand, Anna, and as a surgeon, I need my hands almost more than I need anything else."

The long silence that follows is filled by swishing, clinking, and rattling sounds as Mrs. MacMillan's broom sweeps the last bits of broken glass and dumps them in the can.

Dr. Dan is the first to speak. "Anna, how did you get those cigarette burns on your arm?" He looks over at Mrs. MacMillan. "Did the caseworker mention these to you?"

Anna sharply sucks in air. I slip off the chair in the kitchen and when I reach it, peek around the door frame.

His questions freeze something in me. *Cigarette burns?*

Anna buries her head in her knees and whimpers. I don't hear Pablo come up behind me, when he gently lifts me up and takes me to the couch.

I get on my knees and wrap my arms around my sister, rocking her back and forth.

Mrs. MacMillan walks over and strokes my hair. "She's lucky to have you, Sara."

I am not sure "luck" is the right word. To me, luck is something more sudden than a sister. Luck is like finding a cookie that the rats overlooked.

Or not being called on when you don't know the answer at school.

Or finding Ben and Rachel home when you run away.

That's luck.

When Anna settles down and the glass is all swept and vacuumed, Dr. Dan picks me up and sets me on a counter in the brightly lit kitchen so he can take a closer look at my foot.

"Well, I don't see any glass shavings in the cut, Sara, but just to be safe, I'm going to put some hydrogen peroxide on it. This is going to sting, but only for a moment. You'll see a lot of bubbling around the cut as it cleans it out. Are you ready?"

Anna presses against my leg, clenching her teeth and staring at my foot, like she's the one getting the stinging stuff put on. It's the twin thing I talked about before.

Pablo and Mrs. MacMillan stand in front, giving me

"It will be okay" looks, but I know it won't. Looks try to lie sometimes, but I usually can tell a fib look from a truth one.

"Ready," I answer, not feeling one bit ready. The liquid is cold at first, then turns burning hot around the cut. I yelp, trying to jerk my foot away, but Dr. Dan has a good grip on it.

"Owwowow!" The bubbling starts and the burning fades. Anna and I lean forward and watch the liquid clean the wound.

"All done!" Dr. Dan chirps. "I'll put a Band-Aid on it and you, brave girl, are good to go."

"And as for you, Anna, I have some lotion we can put on your arm that will fade those burn marks."

"No!" Anna presses her other arm across the burned one.

"Good, Anna, for saying 'no.' It doesn't sting," Dr. Dan added quickly. "As a matter of fact, it feels good. Tell you what, I don't even have to put it on. I can just squeeze some lotion in this hand"—he turns the bottle over and pours lotion onto Anna's left hand—"and you can rub it lightly onto your arm. How's that?" He pulls me down from the counter and pats my head.

As Anna rubs the lotion on her burns, a small smile slightly curls her lips. "No hurt!"

Dr. Dan grins. "That's right. No hurt."

But what Anna doesn't see is that Dr. Dan has the hand she bit behind his back, and he's flexing it. Open. Close. Open. Close.

Daddy's hands are important too. He can't play drums if his hands don't work.

Open. Close. Open. Close.

I stare at Dr. Dan's hands, wondering, *Is Daddy okay? Can he come and get us?*

The MacMillans are nice, but I want to go home.

CHAPTER 10

I DON'T HEAR HER COME IN, SO WHEN MRS. MacMillan sits down beside me that evening, there's no trying to hide my tears. All the commotion earlier over the broken plates kept my mind on other things, but now old worries have begun to creep in. Exhausted by the day's events, Anna has fallen asleep on the floor under the window before I can ask her who burned her arm with cigarettes. The thought of someone doing that to her fills me with rage. When her arm falls to the side, I can see the marks make a *P*. I count the circles. There are eight of them.

Mrs. MacMillan hands me a book. "I hear you like

stories," she whispers. "This was one of Pablo's favorites, so I thought you might like it too."

I stare at the cover, not making a move to open it.

She bends down to look at me. "Have you already read it? I can bring you another one, or better yet, why don't you pick one out that you like?"

"This one's fine," I finally answer. I relax, remembering my trick to keep people from knowing I can't read.

"What was your favorite part?" I ask.

"If I tell you that, it will spoil it for you!"

My heart sinks. Most people can't wait to tell me their favorite part of a story, not caring if I've read it or not.

"You read it, then we can compare notes and see if the part you liked best was the one I liked best too!" She raises her eyebrows and grins, like she's expecting an answer.

I don't say anything. It's not like she really asked a question. "I think I know what's troubling you," Mrs. MacMillan says quietly, stroking my hair.

My stomach tightens. "You do?"

She reaches in her pocket and pulls out an envelope. She takes a folded piece of paper out of it. "This fell out of the pocket of your jacket."

Mama's letter! "Did you look at it?" I can barely breathe.

When she nods, my throat tightens even more.

"You miss her, don't you?"

I nod, not believing that she actually read Mama's letter.

She slips the letter back into the envelope and hands it to me. Then she gets up. "Do you want to talk about anything?"

I shake my head and swallow hard. What if she tells Mrs. Craig about the letter? What if they go after Mama? Scared and unsure of what to do, I just sit. "We can talk more later if you like," Mrs. MacMillan says, standing up slowly. "For now, though, try to get a good night's sleep." She kisses the top of my head.

When she leaves, I reach to hide the envelope underneath the bedsheet. Mama's photo falls to the floor. I pick it up, frowning. I stare at the face in the photo. Mama smiles at me like nothing has happened. I wipe hot tears away so I can keep seeing her face.

"Where are you?" I whisper.

I stick the envelope with the letter and photo under the bottom sheet. No one will think to look there. I'll share the picture with Anna later, after everyone has gone to sleep.

As I turn to leave, I spot Pablo's rainmaker where Anna has left it on the dresser. I feel it again. The tug. The feeling that makes me steal things. The noise from the rainmaker calms her. She needs it. That's what I tell myself as I sneak over, carefully pick it up so it won't make any noise, and stuff it under the bottom sheet with Mama's picture and letter.

I grab a blanket from Anna's bed and cover her so she won't get cold.

CHAPTER 11

THE NEXT MORNING, ANNA AND I HEAD DOWN-stairs. Pablo and Dr. Dan have already left for some-where.

But Mrs. MacMillan is sitting in the kitchen, drinking coffee and thumbing through some ads. "Good morning, good morning!" she greets, jumping to her feet. "There are lots of sales going on today. What do you say we go and get you girls some new clothes?"

"Really? New clothes?" I grin at Anna. Most of the clothes I wear are ones that were once hers, and they don't always fit so good.

"You bet! And I know just the store to try first." She

pours us some cereal and milk and lets us look at all the pictures in the ads.

On the way to the store, Anna stares out the window saying nothing. I wiggle in my seat, anxious to get there and see what they have.

The saleslady at the store says she knows just what we want, which is lucky, because Anna and I don't know where to begin. There are so many dresses and pants and shorts and T-shirts and shoes, rows and rows and rows of them all silently shouting, *Pick me! Pick me!* Just like me and Anna at the Silvermans', when Ben could only take one of us to the library

"Don't worry about how much anything costs," Mrs. MacMillan says, breaking into my thoughts. I am trying to read a price tag. I'm better with numbers than with words. Anna is better with words, which is funny, since she hardly talks.

"This is my treat," she adds, holding up a cotton dress. "This will look so good on you!"

We take clothes off, put clothes on, take them off, and put them on, till my ears feel like they're going to fall off from all that pulling.

Finally, we decide on two matching sundresses—one

for me and one for Anna. Mrs. MacMillan also buys us two pairs of shorts with shirts to match, and sandals. My bag alone bulges as round as Big Ed's belly back at the bakery by our real house.

We get in line at the checkout when a lady walks in. I stare, unable to move or speak. It's Mama. I look over at Anna to see if she sees her too, but Anna's too busy thumbing through magazines to notice.

I can't let Mama get away, and race after her.

"I knew you'd come back!" I shout, startling her, judging by how she jolts to a stop and turns, right as I throw my arms around her. "Nobody believed me, but I told them you would come back." She feels different, or maybe I just grew taller in the time she's been gone.

"Honey—" Mrs. MacMillan rushes up and pulls gently at my arm that's still wrapped tightly around Mama.

"I'm so sorry," Mrs. MacMillan tells the lady. "She lost her mother recently—"

"Oh, you poor thing," the woman says, stroking my head.

I jerk back. *That's not Mama's voice.*

I look up. *Mama doesn't have brown eyes.*

"Come back in line, Sara. It was an honest mistake." She tells the stranger sorry again and guides me back to the line. I want to melt. Disappear. Everyone in line is looking at me, whispering to each other.

"Poor thing."

"How sad."

"That woman must have been freaked out, having some strange kid grabbing her."

I drop my head so I don't have to see them. I can still hear them, but something else is screaming in my head: *It was Mama. It was. It was her!* Then another screaming thought tromps all over that one: *What were you thinking? Don't you even know your own mother?*

I try to push that thought away because it makes tears crop up from nowhere, stinging my eyes. I can't wait to get out of the store. I will never come to this stupid store ever, ever again.

When we reach the car, I scramble in the back while Mrs. MacMillan and Anna put the packages in the trunk. When Mrs. MacMillan gets in, she cranks her head around and looks at me. "Are you okay?"

I look out the window and don't say anything.

"I've had that happen before. Thought someone

was somebody else. Our minds can play tricks on us."

I don't want to think about it anymore, and keep staring out the window. She turns back, starts the car, and finally gets us away from there.

The drive back to the MacMillans' is silent, except for the *pop, pop, pop* as Anna yanks Abby apart.

When we pull into the driveway, Mrs. MacMillan grins. "Oh, good. The boys are back." She turns to look over the seat and says, "So long as you don't stray too far, you can take a look around the neighborhood and maybe meet some of the other kids on the block.

"They're usually at the park at the end of the street," she adds. "Dan and I will come and get you in about fifteen minutes."

A bit of space sounds great. I quickly pop Anna's doll back together and hand it to her. She says, "Bathroom," and I nod. I'll wait.

When she comes back out, she sees Sneaker under a bush and scoops her up, carrying the cat in one hand, Abby in the other.

There are only a few kids in the park when we get there. Anna holds back and sticks close to a tree. Sneaker, I can tell, wants to get down.

"Run away?"

I look back at her. "You mean Sneaker? I don't think so. She just wants to explore with us."

"I'll wait here." Anna sits down and starts pulling Abby apart. New settings are hard for her to get used to.

The kids see us and run over. One boy, who looks to be about nine, scoops Sneaker up and rubs his cheek against her coat.

"My cat!" Anna yells. It's the first time I've seen her yell at someone she doesn't know. I grin. Maybe she can stand up for herself after all.

"I'm just petting him," the boy says, eyeing Abby. "Hey, what's with the busted doll?"

I look at the scattered pieces of Abby on the grass and back at the boy. "We're playing a game," I tell him, covering up for Anna's strange habit.

"What's the game? Pick up limbs?" The boy laughs, making the other kids laugh too. He bends down and picks up an arm piece and turns to his friends. "Need a hand, anyone?"

Again they all laugh.

"Give back!" Anna jumps to her feet and hooks an arm around the boy's neck, pulling him back against her and squeezing until his face looks puffy and red. His breathing sounds pinched and eerie.

"Anna!" I run over and try to pull her arm off. "Anna, let go! You're choking him! Let go, Anna! Let go!"

The boy grows limp, and when Anna finally releases him, he falls to the ground. He doesn't move.

"You killed him," his friends shout.

"What's going on here?"

I whirl around. When I see Dr. Dan, I almost start to cry. "Anna got upset. This boy made fun of her doll, and she choked him. Now he's not breathing."

Dr. Dan drops down beside the limp boy, sits him up, and thumps him on the back with a cupped hand. Like magic, the kid opens his eyes, coughs a few times, and looks around like he's wondering where he is. Anna just stares blankly, as if she doesn't know what all the fuss is about.

Dr. Dan ruffles the boy's hair. "He's going to be all right," he says, checking the boy's eyes. I can tell he's mad at Anna, but he doesn't say anything to her. Maybe he doesn't want to get bitten again, because all he says is, "Can you kids show me where he lives? Anna and Sara, why don't you go home with Barbara?"

We watch them walk away, Dr. Dan carrying the boy, the others clustered around him. I spin around and glare at Anna.

"You could have killed him. What were you thinking?"

She bends over and starts picking up doll parts. Mrs. MacMillan squats down to help.

"Would you want to be choked?" Why can't she just be like a normal sister and answer a question?

"Sara—I think Anna's had enough stress for one day."

I ignore Mrs. MacMillan, keeping my glare glued to Anna. "Do you want people to hate us? Is that why you're so mean? Biting. Spitting. And now, almost choking a kid? Keep it up, Anna, and nobody will want us around. *Nobody*."

"Sara—please." Mrs. MacMillan stands up, holding arms, legs, a head, and a body. "Please, sweetheart, give Anna some thinking room."

Anna rises to her feet and looks at me with a look so blank that a chill chases up my arm. Then she does something she's never done before. She walks away.

"Go ahead. Run away, Anna. Be like Mama. I don't care. You hear me? I don't care." Tears burn my eyes.

Mrs. MacMillan rushes ahead to catch up with

Anna, calling for me to follow, but I stay rooted to my spot, stewing in anger. Why can't she just be normal?

Anna's head hangs low. Mrs. MacMillan must have asked if she could put an arm around her, because Anna nods and Mrs. MacMillan wraps an arm around Anna's shoulder.

I start to head after them, when I hear footsteps and turn around to see Dr. Dan coming up behind me. He falls into pace. "The boy's going to be fine, Sara." We walk a while, listening to the crunching of our feet on the ground. We pass Anna and Mrs. MacMillan. "Tough day, huh?"

"You don't know the half of it." I lower my voice, looking over my shoulder at my sister. "Sometimes I wish she would just go away." I feel his hand settle lightly on my shoulder. I look up, expecting to see Daddy's "I'm here, don't worry" face and look away quickly when I see Dr. Dan's instead. My mind tricks me again, making me forget Daddy's gone. I stare at the ground and pretend that it's Daddy beside me trying to make me feel better, and not someone trying to be Daddy.

"Every now and again we all have feelings like that,"

he says in a voice so different from Daddy's that it becomes hard to pretend anymore.

"Who do you want to go away?" I wonder if he'll say, "You and Anna," but he doesn't.

"With me, it's not about who and more about what I want to go away. And what I want to go away is disease."

This time I don't look at him. Everyone wants different things. I stare at the grass as we cross the yard, glancing back at my footprints, softly outlined. They'll be gone before we reach the house.

When the front door opens, I hear the phone ringing. It turns out that Mrs. Craig has good news and bad. The bad news is that they still don't have a home for us. The good news is that we don't have to go back to the Cottages. The Silvermans are going to take us back until we can be placed with a more permanent family.

While Mrs. MacMillan talks with Mrs. Craig, Anna and I help set the table. I put the napkins at each place. The one extra I stick in my pocket in case Anna and I get hungry later.

Dr. Dan then gathers us around the dinner table and talks about the family's upcoming trip to South

America. While he talks, he serves each of us a plate of tamales, corn, salad, chips, and salsa.

I'm still mad at Anna, so I don't look at her or pass her a plate.

"I've been with this particular team for six years," Dr. Dan says. "I was shocked to hear Dr. Bentley got sick and they needed me to come so soon. But there are so many children who need help right away."

"*Podemos ayudar,*" Pablo says.

I stare at him.

"That was Spanish for 'We can help,'" he explains. "Spanish is my native tongue."

Native tongue. The words sound strange next to each other. "I don't speak anything but English. Guess nobody would understand me if I went to Chile."

"Oh, I don't know about that." Dr. Dan smiles. "You'd be surprised at what people can understand. It doesn't always take words to say something. The look on your face, the sound of your voice—those are the things that matter. A simple smile can go a long way." He pushes his dinner plate back and pats his stomach. "Well, I don't know about you guys, but I'm full."

"Not too full to repair the upstairs bathroom, I hope,"

Mrs. MacMillan says, helping herself to more salad.

Dr. Dan groans. "It's amazing how one small leak can cause so much trouble."

Well, he's right about that. Anna didn't wet the bed last night, so they probably don't know about her little problem, but one little leak does cause a lot of trouble.

"You girls must be excited about going back to the Silvermans'," Mrs. MacMillan says as Pablo and Dr. MacMillan head upstairs to work on the plumbing. "And you'll have brand-new clothes to take with you," she adds.

"Thanks again for the nice clothes," I mumble. I'm not ready to be un-mad at Anna yet. Anna mumbles, "Thanks." I wonder if she feels as torn as I do about leaving. We're just starting to get used to the MacMillans. Pablo is the big brother we never had, and he can speak two languages! Mrs. MacMillan is nice and really seems to like us. Dr. Dan goes to faraway places to help kids. Their world is a bigger place than Anna and I have ever known, maybe ever will know. Still, as big as it is, it isn't big enough for Anna and me to fit in it.

"Sneaker?" Anna looks hopeful, but Mrs. MacMillan shakes her head.

"If you're talking about Sneaker coming with you, I'm sorry, sweetie. No cats. Mrs. Craig said that maybe when you get into a more permanent setting you can have a pet, but this isn't a good time. I did ask, though."

"Will you be taking Sneaker with you?" I look up at Mrs. MacMillan, already knowing the answer.

"I can't lie to you, Sara. We won't be taking Sneaker."

"When will Mrs. Craig come and get us?" I ask, crushed that Sneaker can't come with us. I know I'll have to find a place to hide her so she won't get hurt or picked up by Animal Control.

"Mrs. Craig will be here early tomorrow morning."

"That soon? I thought we were going to stay here longer." I slump in my chair.

"I thought so too, honey. But something has come up. A baby was born who's very sick, and now that the other doctor is sick too, we're going to have to leave for South America sooner than we'd expected."

Anna sits and stares at her doll.

Mrs. MacMillan turns to the sink and starts running water and washing dishes. I follow Anna back to the table and sit across from her.

"It's your fault that we have to move. I hope you know that," I whisper.

Anna's stone face never changes expression. It's like she doesn't even hear me. "New plans," she blurts hotly.

"Yeah, they have new plans, or so they say, but after you practically choked that kid to death, they probably made up all that sick-baby stuff so they can get rid of us sooner. You're the reason nobody wants us, Anna. Nobody. Not even Mama or Daddy."

"No like Anna?" she whispers. *Pop, pop, pop.* Doll parts fall to the floor until I want to reach across with my foot and smash every last one of them.

"Life would be so much better—" I don't finish the sentence. I don't need to.

Anna pulls Abby's head off and hurls it across the room.

That night, I can't sleep. How can I have said all those things to Anna? I sound just like Mama when she told me, "You're just like him," and then ran away.

Anna can't help the way she is. I wonder if what happened to her when we got separated that one time was what changed her. It's as if when she got burned with the cigarettes, fear got burned into her. She's like two people now. The Outside Anna and Inside Anna. I want the inside one, my sister, back. But still, inside . . . outside . . . I can't shake the thought that she's the real reason—not some job or sick baby—that we have to leave.

CHAPTER 12

WHEN I ROLL OVER AND LOOK AT MY SISTER, the moon casts a soft white glow against her skin. She looks so peaceful. So normal. I feel horrible all over again for getting so mad at her, and for saying I wished she would go away. And just like that, things change as she slips into a nightmare and starts thrashing and crying out.

"Anna. Anna! Wake up." She wakes up crying so hard, she wets the bed. That makes her cry even harder.

"Shhh." I reach under the bottom sheet and grab the rainmaker to comfort her. When she's calm, I tell her how I'll get new sheets. "You see if you can find a box or something we can put these in." I pile the soiled fitted sheet and top sheet up next to the bed. I've seen where Mrs. MacMillan keeps linens, in a hall closet, and I hurriedly tiptoe out to grab replacement sheets.

When I come back, I hear Anna's whimpers coming from a corner.

"Did you find a box?"

She sniffs loudly and holds one up that she found in the closet. Drawn on it is a birthday cake with candles. Probably left over from Pablo's last birthday. I hand Anna the clean sheets and wad up the damp ones. While I stuff them into the box, she puts the new sheets on the bed. "No one will know," I tell her. "It'll be our secret."

When we're done, I tuck her into bed. "I'll be right back. I have to find a good place to hide the box."

She nods and pulls the sheet up tight around her chin.

On tiptoe, I sneak into Pablo's room, hesitating at the attic door. It has a different kind of knob than other doors in the house. It isn't a knob at all, really. More like a small silver handle that clicks loudly when I turn it. Pablo's lucky to have an attic room right off his bedroom.

Pablo stirs in his bed but doesn't wake up. My heart pounds so hard. I set the box down quietly and slowly pull the door open, breathing through each creak, hoping Pablo won't catch me.

Once inside, I notice that the empty attic is surprisingly cool. Feeling my way along the wall with my elbow, I put the box in a corner and then feel my way (this time with my hands) back to the door, latching it behind me.

As I tiptoe across the room, I feel big like a giant, when I want to feel like a mouse—small and invisible. I watch Pablo, hoping he stays asleep, and run headlong into Mrs. MacMillan.

"So, you're the little mouse I hear moving around," she whispers. My heart races. Did she see me go in the attic? Will she find the hidden sheets?

"You scared the living daylights out of me," she adds.

I have no clue what living daylights are, but judging by her face, I know she's shaken.

"I couldn't sleep," I mumble. "I was checking to see if Pablo was awake." It isn't the total truth, but it isn't a total lie, either. After all, I was looking to see if he was awake when I bumped into her.

"Next time you can't sleep, wake me up."

I look up and nod, thinking, *I did wake you up*, but don't say anything. She leads me back to my bedroom, where Anna sits wide-eyed, looking scared. I crawl in beside her.

"Goodness! You can't sleep either?" Mrs. MacMillan sits on the edge of the bed closest to me.

Anna glances my way, and I smile and nod a tiny nod so she'll know our secret is safe. Relieved, Anna looks back at Mrs. MacMillan and shakes her head.

"I know you're excited about going to the Silvermans', but you need your rest. Ruth—Mrs. Craig, that is—will be here bright and early."

"I still don't see why you and Dr. Dan can't keep us," I blurt out. "I mean, we got here before you heard about the sick baby."

Mrs. MacMillan looks first at Anna, then at me. She takes a deep breath and lets it out slowly. "Mrs. Craig told you this was only a temporary placement, Sara, while they tried to find a more permanent home, right?"

"But she always says that. I thought you guys liked us and might want to keep us." I squeeze my hands into fists to keep from crying.

"We do like you, but this isn't about liking. It's about commitment. Doctors Without Borders is something we committed to years ago. It's our way of making the world a better place. We opened our home so you would have a place to stay, but we're foster parents, Sara. We weren't thinking about adopting."

"You adopted Pablo," I remind her hotly.

"That was different. No one told us we couldn't adopt him. But with you—" She stares at her fingers as she twists them together.

"Well, there are strings attached. Your parents are keeping anyone from adopting you. Your mother is nowhere to be found, and your father—"

I lie still, hardly daring to breathe. The air around me feels ice-cold, like it would crack if I even moved a muscle.

"It's great that your daddy is trying so hard to hold on, but it makes it hard for a family to adopt you."

"Daddy's holding on to us because he's coming back." My arms are crossed over my chest so tightly that I can hardly breathe. Still, it gives my body a sense that something's holding it together. I'm afraid that if I let go, I might just spill out all over the place.

She tucks the sheet around us. "I hope you're right, Sara. It's hard for us to leave, not knowing if you girls have found a home with parents who can be there for you."

"So you're really going?" I look up, hoping she might change her mind.

"Yes, we're going, but that is not to say we aren't going to miss you both terribly." She leans over and kisses my forehead. "I've been nothing but honest with you, right?"

I nod, even though I'm thinking that honesty doesn't always mean anything feels better. It's as if she reads my thoughts.

"I know the truth can hurt, but I also believe that being honest and open and keeping one's word are important ways to show love for each other. I could easily make things up. But I want you to be able to believe what I say and to know that I'm not trying to hurt you. I'm just trying to let you know in advance how things will be so you're not caught off guard. Does that make sense?"

I nod, wanting to make her feel better about leaving us. It's not her fault that Dr. Dan's on this team and they can't stay. And she did take good care of us. Still . . .

As she moves toward my sister, Anna curls up into a tight ball and hides her head.

"Good night, Anna." She tucks the sheets around her. "Think good thoughts," she says, looking at me, then leaves.

Anna uncurls and pokes her head out. "Sheets all gone?" she whispers.

"The attic was empty, so there's no reason for anyone to go in there. It's safe, Anna."

With that, she slips into a relaxed sleep while I stare at the spiderlike shadows on the wall. I make a circle around the shadows with my fingers. It looks like a dream catcher. But the shadow dream catcher is not real enough to pull bad thoughts away. I roll onto my side and think about what Mrs. MacMillan said.

There are strings attached. Was she saying Mama and Daddy have us tied to some invisible string? Are we like kites?

I picture big scissors hovering over us. *Snip, snip.* Everyone knows what happens when kite strings get cut.

Bye-bye, kites.

CHAPTER 13

THE NEXT MORNING, WE WAKE UP AND HEAR Dr. Dan and Mrs. MacMillan talking to Mrs. Craig, who has already arrived to get us. Anna and I race to get our clothes on.

Clutching Abby, Anna starts for the door.

"Wait. We can't forget Mama's picture." I reach under the sheets. Mama's letter and picture are gone! I yank on the mattress and hold it up for Anna to look. She shakes her head. Not again!

I gasp. "What could have happened to them?" We search the top of the bed, under it, under the covers, inside the pillow covers. No photo. No letter. No nothing.

"And where's Cowwy?" I wail. We search and search,

but there is no sign of Cowwy, either. It's as if a ghost sneaked in during the night and snatched them.

"Pablo!" I cry.

"Pablo?" Anna looks at me all funny.

"Don't you see? He's getting back at me because I stole his stupid rainmaker." I look around for it, but it, too, has disappeared.

I march downstairs, Anna right behind me, furious with Pablo.

"You stole rainmaker?"

I ignore Anna's question. Everyone is waiting at the car. I dump our bags in the backseat.

"Well, girls, are you ready?" Mrs. MacMillan sounds chipper, but she has dark circles under her eyes.

"They're pretty tired," she explains to Mrs. Craig. "Last night—" Her voice trails off. I glance at Anna, who looks sadder than ever. Her half-heart necklace hangs limply over her shirt. I reach up to touch mine. It's gone.

"My necklace!"

"Did you lose something?" Pablo looks at me. How dare he pretend not to know what's wrong! I turn away, not saying anything about Cowwy, Mama's letter, the photo, or the necklace. What does he want with a necklace, a letter, a photo, and a stuffed animal? He's just being mean.

"You lost your necklace?" Mrs. MacMillan looks alarmed. "Let's go search your room. Maybe it fell on the carpet."

Soon everyone is up in the room on hands and knees, searching.

I crawl over to Pablo. "You are going to look pretty dumb in a girl's necklace," I whisper. "And what do you want with a letter that's not even addressed to you?" There. Now he knows that I know. I could maybe get another necklace, but Mama's letter and picture?

To my surprise, he isn't giving me the "You caught me" look I'm expecting. Instead, he leans close and whispers, "When you cheat, or lie, or steal, everything you do reflects it, like a mirror."

Now, what is that supposed to mean? I'm not looking into any mirror. "You should know," I snap.

I crawl back over to Anna. We've lost Mama's letter, her photo, the necklace, and Cowwy. Maybe if I had given Pablo his stupid rainmaker back—

Anna lets out a sharp cry and holds up a broken

strand of necklace chain. But we can't find the rest of the necklace anywhere. And now, ready or not, it's time to go.

"I'm so sorry, girls, but we really must get going," Mrs. Craig says, gently gripping my shoulders and pointing me to the door.

I whip around. "We can't go! We can't just leave the necklace behind. Mama gave me that. It's all I have of her."

"I just don't know where it could be, Sara," Mrs. MacMillan says.

"I do!" I glare at Pablo, stomping past him toward the car.

"Such sad faces!" Dr. Dan bends down, twists his eyebrows, and puckers his mouth, trying, I think, to get us to laugh.

"Good-byes are never easy," Mrs. Craig announces. I'm thinking that when you have to say them often enough, they seem to get a whole lot easier. She starts the engine. "We'd better get rolling! I have to be in court at ten thirty."

I'm getting pretty good at figuring out who expects a hug, who just wants words, and who's waiting to shake our hands. No way is Pablo getting a hug. Not after what he did.

"See ya," I say, when it comes his turn.

He walks over to Anna's side of the car.

"I have something for you," he tells her. Anna's eyes brighten when she sees the rainmaker. "Now every time it rains, I'll know who to thank!" He ducks down and looks over at me.

He stole the rainmaker back? The thief!

"And here's something for you, too, Sara." I don't want to look, but then I get to wondering about the necklace, Cowwy, and Mama's letter, and her photo, and I think maybe he's going to give back what he stole. He doesn't. Instead, he hands me a box.

I look up at him, puzzled. "What's this?"

"Look in it," he answers as we pull away.

I look in it, hoping to see everything I am sure he took. It's empty, except for a mirror and a dancer that twirls round and round, playing a tinny little song. As we drive off, I twist around and look back at the house. I bet Mrs. MacMillan doesn't even know she adopted a robber.

"Oh no! My jacket! I forgot my jacket! We have to

go back." I look at Mrs. Craig, hoping she'll turn the car around.

"There's no time, Sara. We can get you another one."

I collapse against the seat and close my eyes. How could so much of me get left behind? First Mama, then Daddy, then Mama's letter and her photo, then Cowwy, then my half-heart necklace, and now my jacket.

All of them—gone.

"I know that tune!" Mrs. Craig says, and she starts singing, "Raindrops keep falling on my head. . . ."

I close the box, and it stops playing. She doesn't stop singing, though. It's like someone wound her up.

CHAPTER 14

I DON'T KNOW WHO'S HAPPIER, THE SILVERMANS seeing us or us seeing them, but the smiles and hugs are big and real. For a while I can forget all the things that got left behind.

"I don't want to go and spoil everyone's good time," Mrs. Craig announces, "but it's important you both understand that this move is only—"

"Temporary!" I shout. Maybe I should get a T-shirt with the word stamped in huge letters across it.

Mrs. Craig cups her hand under my chin and tilts my head up. "I have some news," she says. "Let's sit under the tree and talk a few minutes."

Mrs. Craig, taking time to sit and talk? Something is wrong. Something is very, very wrong.

A silent signal seems to pass between Mrs. Craig and the Silvermans. One minute they're standing there, the next they're grabbing our things and heading for the house.

As we watch the Silvermans shuffle across the yard, Anna clutches my hand. When they are out of sight, Mrs. Craig lets out a long sigh. That right there says it all. The news is bad.

"It's about your father," she says, and my stomach knots up. "He's free now, but the judge has put a restraining order on him."

"A restraining order? What do you mean, a restraining order?" I demand. Anna tightens her grip.

"He is not to see you girls until he gets some help for his drinking problem, his temper, and a few other things he has to deal with. The judge will review his case after he completes rehabilitation and parenting classes. But I have to be honest with both of you. Based on his record, it's not looking good. I'm so sorry," she adds, sounding like she means it.

I can hear Anna sniffing, but I don't look at her. She

lets go of my hand and starts pounding Abby against the grass. Mrs. Craig catches her arms and gently but firmly pulls Anna into a hug. Anna starts squirming, but Mrs. Craig doesn't let go. She just keeps rocking and talking, rocking and talking, soothing the hurt.

I can't look. Sometimes bad news has a way of wrapping around me so tight, I can hardly breathe. I feel something crawling on my leg and look down. A caterpillar is inching up my shin toward my knee. I watch it through a blur, knowing that someday soon it will change into a butterfly. Things can change for the better. That's what the caterpillar is trying to tell me. Things can change for the better. The question is, Can Daddy? The judge is saying no. But maybe the judge is wrong. Maybe Daddy can be like the caterpillar and change.

When Anna has no more fight left in her, Mrs. Craig tells us more. "What this means is that the judge will now consider allowing a family to adopt you. That way, you won't have to keep moving from one family to another." She's looking at me like she's waiting for an answer. I just sit, watching the caterpillar crawl from my knee to the hand that's resting on my leg.

"I know not being with your dad is hard to imagine

right now, but doesn't a permanent home with permanent parents sound like something you've always wanted?"

It's a hard question to answer. Saying yes feels like we're turning our backs on Mama and Daddy, but saying no would mean we like jumping from house to house. So again, I don't say anything. That way no one can get hurt.

I let the caterpillar crawl onto the grass, and then I gather up Abby's arms and legs, like I always do, and pop them back into place. I hand my sister her doll.

Mrs. Craig grunts as she pushes herself up from the grass and nods to Ben and Rachel, who cross the yard toward us. "I'll call in a couple of days to see how you're doing," she says.

I don't even have to look up to know she's checking the time. I watch her drive away, feeling empty inside.

CHAPTER 15

"HOW ABOUT A WALK TO CLEAR OUR HEADS?"
Ben suggests. He has his walking shoes on. Anna and I
nod. Rachel says she needs to rest, so it's just me, Anna,
and Ben.

The fresh air feels good. I breathe in deep and let
the air blow my thoughts around. At one point, it feels
like someone's watching us, but when I turn around
and look down the street, I don't see anyone or anything
strange. A truck and some cars are parked by the side of
the road, but nothing looks out of place. Some people
are walking their dogs.

My thoughts drift to Mrs. Craig's news. I don't want
to go to another house. I want to stay here, with the

Silvermans. It's no secret that they can't keep us. Why do they have to be so old?

I keep thinking about being adopted. Becoming a part of a family with a mom and dad who are always there. Can something like that really happen to me and Anna?

I sigh. Maybe we should just run away again. But where would we go? If only we knew where Mama was. Would she even want us?

I have this awful feeling that I'll find her and do something wrong, and she'll look at me like she isn't even surprised. "You're just like your daddy," she'd probably say, and leave again.

"Ruth told me what happened with your papa," Ben says, wrapping an arm around my shoulder. "I know it is not something you wanted to hear."

"Daddy will get better," I assure him. "He'll get us back, you'll see."

"It is not easy what your papa has to overcome, Sara. Drinking is not an easy thing to get over."

"Daddy will choose us over drinking," I answer, careful not to echo Ben and say the words "drinking" and "thing" like they end with a *k*.

SARA LOST AND FOUND

"I know he wants to, but sometimes something gets hold of us that is not good for us. We convince ourselves we can handle it. But we can't. It's called an addiction. And your papa has this addiction." He grows quiet.

"Sara," Anna says softly.

I study my sister's face. Her chin is trembling. She has the same look as when we thought a burglar had broken into the house. But what can be scaring her? We're with Ben. We're safe.

Ben stops to rest at a bench and invites us to sit down, but Anna won't sit.

"She hears something," I explain.

Ben looks at her thoughtfully. "I hear something too, Anna. Birds. The wind. A siren—hear it? An ice cream truck."

I grin. For an old man with a hearing aid, Ben sure is hearing a lot.

"Are you making that up?" I look closely at his face for a sign that he's teasing.

"Maybe I am, but you hear them too, don't you?"

I nod. The siren is getting closer. *Wait! Is someone calling my name?*

Ben jumps up from the park bench and stands

straighter and stiffer than I've ever seen him stand. The expression on his face is grim and set. Something is wrong.

"Sara! Over here!" a voice yells.

I turn and see him. At first I think it's a man who looks like Daddy who just happens to be driving a pickup like his. Maybe my mind is playing tricks on me again. But then, when he says my name again, I start to run toward him. "Daddy!"

I never see the car coming from the other direction.

"No!" Anna's scream pierces the air like an animal in pain. I stop, as if someone jerked a collar around my neck and pulled back. The car swerves and misses me.

The next thing I know, Ben is pulling me off the street to the side of the road. Cars are screeching to a stop.

"Find me, Anna. Sara. You're Olsons. Never forget that. You're Olsons!" His words disappear with his truck around a corner.

The police siren grows closer. Through the blur, I see the officer stop and run over to us.

"He never even stopped to make sure they were okay," Ben shouts.

I get up, but the policeman makes me rest on the curb until he's sure we're both okay. Anna sits beside me, rubbing her elbow, staring blankly in the direction Daddy had driven. She fell running after me.

While Ben talks with the policeman, I talk to Anna. "You okay?" I look up into her face. The fear-twin thing passes between us and I put my arm around her. Daddy's words still ring in my ears, but they feel more like a warning than a comfort.

"Being an Olson isn't easy," I finally whisper.

"Not easy," Anna agrees.

Minutes later, Ben reaches down and we both grab his hands, pulling ourselves up to our feet.

CHAPTER 16

ANNA AND I ARE LOST IN THOUGHT ON THE WAY back to the Silvermans'.

No broken bones. Just a lot of bruises. I swallow hot tears. Ben walks between us and puts his arm over each of our shoulders. He rocks side to side, murmuring soothing words in Russian. It doesn't matter that we can't understand the words. Their meaning is clear.

When we get to the Silvermans', I wince while stepping up and into the house. I feel like Daddy's truck did run me over.

That night Mrs. Silverman makes our favorite meal, chicken with mashed potatoes and peas.

"Nothing like a good chicken leg to round out a

meal," Ben says, trying, I think, to keep things light.

"Round out your belly, you mean," Rachel answers, flitting around the table like a mother bird.

"That, too!" Ben agrees. I grin as he rubs his stomach.

Everyone is trying not to talk about it, but Daddy is out there somewhere, running from the law.

Finally, Rachel leans over and looks into my face. "You miss your papa. I know this. But it was not right the way he called to you. You could have by that car gotten killed! The courts told him to stay away."

"Then I hate the courts," I say. "He's our daddy!"

"He needs to work out some things." She says the word "work" as if it starts with a *v*. "Like, for instance, his drinking. He is the papa. He is supposed to take care of you. Not the other way around. So the courts, they find you a new home with a mama and papa who will look after you."

I cry so hard there aren't any more tears to fall. "Mama said when she looks at me she sees Daddy," I cry out. "That's why she ran away."

Rachel puts down the plates she's carrying and sits beside me. "Is this what you are thinking all the time?

That it is your fault your mama and papa are having these troubles?"

I don't answer, but I don't need to. Rachel knows.

"Ah, *kia*. Poor baby. You are not just like your papa. You are you, Sara. And Anna is Anna. Loving girls. Caring sisters. Maybe your mama, she just meant you look like your papa. You sing like him. I think this must be what she was meaning. She was talking about the good things. Maybe she thinks things would be better if she went away and tried to find work. She loves you girls. I just know it. Your papa loves you too. It's just that sometimes in life, we can't always be with the ones we love for one reason or another. It has nothing to do with you. You were in the middle caught. Can you understand this?"

I shrug.

"Now something else is bothering you. What is this thing that eats you up inside?"

Secrets are getting harder and harder to hide. Maybe Anna isn't the problem. Maybe I am. "I steal things," I whisper. "That's why nobody wants me. Wants us," I add.

"What things you steal? Money?"

I shake my head.

"Then what things?"

"Paper towels—rainmakers." My head grows heavy.

Anna and Rachel both stare at me a long time. "And did you feel good about taking these things?"

I wonder for a moment if the racing of my heartbeat that I feel while stealing is the same as feeling good. I decide it isn't and shake my head.

"And did you tell somebody how sorry you are?"

I hesitate. I didn't exactly tell Pablo I was sorry.

"Have you done anything nice since then?" she prods.

I nod.

"Well, then, I say next time you feel like stealing, you stop and ask, 'Is this what my heart wants to do?'" She makes a line from her head to her heart. "You stop again. You ask, 'Is this what my head wants to do?' If your heart, it says one thing, and your head, it says another? You don't do. You see how this works? Line up head and heart." She taps her forehead and draws a line down to her heart, and then points to her feet. "You do this and your feet, they will follow. Those nice things you said you did can be the stars on your chart in here." She taps her heart. "To replace the marks for stealing. Yes?"

"Yes," I whisper.

"You have learned from this?"

I nod.

"Then forgive yourself and try not to do again." She gives me a hug. Her voice drops to almost a whisper. "You made these choices to steal, yes, but not for bad reasons. This does not make them right, but you were trying to look after your sister, yes?"

My cheek rubs against her dress as I nod. I feel her strong heartbeat against my ear.

Rachel then holds out her arms to Anna, inviting her into a hug. Instead of shrinking away, Anna rushes into her arms and holds on so tight, I have to look away to keep from crying.

Finally, Rachel holds her at arm's length and asks, "You have secrets to talk about too, Anna?"

Anna looks at me, remembering, I'm sure, how she almost choked a boy to death and all the times she's wet the bed. She shakes her head.

CHAPTER 17

WHEN THE DAY IS FINALLY OVER AND WE'VE had baths, brushed our teeth, and crawled into bed, Ben comes in with a book. "Anyone for a story?"

Anna and I both nod. Anything to get my mind off the bad news about Daddy. And the fact that Mrs. Craig had told Rachel that she had a new, temporary foster home for us. Plus, we love Ben's stories. Sometimes he just tells one off the top of his head. Other times he reads. But when he reads, it's always from the same book.

"*The Magic Journey*," he begins, opening to the middle.

"Shouldn't you start at the beginning?" I ask, just as I ask every time he reads a story from his book.

His eyes dance. "Ah, but remember, this is *The Magic Journey*, and in a magic journey, you can start anywhere. At the beginning, at the middle, at the end. It matters not."

He clears his throat. "I begin now the tale of the Nine-Story Cat."

"Big cat," Anna murmurs, flashing a quick smile.

Ben laughs. "Well, bighearted, maybe. Actually, it's the building it lives in that's big.

"The story goes that a young cat named Faith, of all things, lived on the ground floor of an old, old building, built hundreds of years—if not more—ago."

I strain to look at the page, but Ben holds the book close to his chest. "Just use your mind's eye, Sara. No need to look at pictures here"—he points to the book—"when you have them here." He points to his head. I relax against the pillow and listen.

"Now, word was out that something mysterious— something magical, even—lived at the very top of this nine-story building. This something was beyond all somethings that could be imagined by any of the cats living in and around the building. At the top was a place nobody had ever seen.

"'It's probably haunted,' said one cat. Tabby was his name. He was a bushy-tailed, arrogant sort that walked around with his head high in the air.

"'You think so?' said Faith. She looked up, wondering if it could be any scarier there than it was right where she was living—struggling to find food and a safe corner to sleep in every night.

"'I heard,' said Eve, who was a short-haired alley cat, 'that a garden more beautiful than any we have ever seen is waiting, filled with sweet-smelling flowers, yummy birds, and no dogs!'

"'We know of no one who has made it all the way to the top,' said Tabby, plucking at one of his nails. 'Though I made it once to the seventh floor. I was lucky to make it out alive. There were rats the size of German shepherds. Snakes longer than any telephone cord you have ever played with.' He shuddered, and all the cats huddled around him to hear more. All except Faith, who had decided that it was time to go find out for herself what was up there. She was tired of being scared of something she couldn't see.

"Tabby had chosen to climb the stairs floor by floor, facing whatever lay ahead. But after hearing of all the awful things he encountered along the way, Faith decided she would take the elevator and just go right to the top.

"As the old elevator groaned and moaned up and up and up, Faith's heart began to beat faster and faster. What would greet her when the doors opened?

"The elevator stopped. Faith's heart beat so fast she thought she might faint. Slowly, the doors parted. Faith stepped out, and before she could run back in, the big elevator doors closed behind her with a *thud*. And there, on the top floor of the nine-story building, Faith found herself face-to-face—" Ben pauses and looks at us, eyes wide and sparkly, before going on. "She found herself face-to-face with a great big lioness!"

"A lioness!" Anna and I hug one another. "She didn't eat her, did she?"

"Well, that's the funny thing." Ben looks at us out of the corner of his eye. "Lionesses are the hunters in the family, and the lions are the protectors, but she didn't eat the kitten. Instead, the lioness roared, showing all her sharp teeth. Faith was scared, but she roared too, only her roar came out sounding a little more like a meow. Still, a roar is a roar.

"Then the mighty lioness slashed the air with her paw and began to pace. Faith also slashed the air with her paw and paced right along with her. But don't be fooled. While Faith was doing all this roaring and slashing and pacing, she was trembling inside. The last thing she wanted to be was this lioness's snack.

"Finally, the lioness settled down, curled up on the floor, and looked at Faith with sleepy eyes. Exhausted, Faith stretched out as well and, light as a feather, pawed at her great paw. The lioness purred.

"Then Faith rubbed her small head against the lioness's large one, and the big cat purred even louder. But something seemed strange. Faith wasn't rubbing something. She was touching something smooth like glass, and it was cool. Faith stood back and looked again. This wasn't a lioness! It was a mirror!

"It had been a reflection of herself."

"Faith is a nine-story cat!" Anna squeals, but all I can think about is when Pablo said, "When you cheat, or lie, or steal, everything you do reflects it, like a mirror."

"Stay with us, Sara!" Ben coaxes, smiling.

"Faith stood tall," he continues. "She felt different now, not the frightened little cat she had once been.

And when she looked out the window, the world looked different too. For the first time, she could see how everything, even the cluster of cats gathered in the park below, were all part of a much grander picture—a picture she would never have seen had she not had the courage to go on this little journey.

"So, you see? It was scary for her, but Faith looked into a mirror and, for the first time, saw someone strong and confident looking back.

"And that, my two sleepy princesses, is the story of the Nine-Story Cat."

I drop back onto my pillow, not wanting Ben's story to end. "Can you tell us another?"

Ben kisses us good night. "What I should do is teach you girls to read. Then you could discover a whole world of stories."

The shock of his words hits like a bucket of ice water dumping on my head. "You know we can't read?" I sit up, stunned that he knows my best-kept secret. How did he find out?

"It's nothing to be ashamed of, Sara. Reading is something you can learn, and when you do, you'll look at the world differently. You'll see."

All this talk about reading reminds me of Mama's lost letter and how Anna and I will never know what Mama wrote in it. I sink against the pillow.

"Ah-ah. No sad thoughts before you go to bed," Ben says, brushing a frown from my forehead. "Only good thoughts before you sleep. Always think good thoughts."

"Sneaker okay?" Anna is sitting on the edge of the bed, swinging her legs. Her pink flannel nightgown has little green flowers all over it. She pokes a finger through a buttonhole. It's morning. We've just finished breakfast and are getting dressed. Mrs. Craig called to say that she's on her way over to take us to our new foster home.

"I don't know if she is or not," I answer, surprising myself. Usually I make something up so she'll feel better. "I hope she's okay." I sigh.

When Mrs. Craig arrives and says she's ready to take us, Anna and I refuse to come downstairs.

"Anna! Sara! All this way she has come, and you hide on the steps?" Rachel scolds.

I know Anna's feeling what I'm feeling. Ben once told us that if we ever get scared, we should go to a place in our minds that's safe—a place where no one can hurt us. I realize that the safest place of all is here at the Silvermans'. The very place we can't stay.

When we reach the bottom of the stairs, Rachel ushers us to the kitchen. "You and the girls should help yourselves to doughnuts," she says to Mrs. Craig. "I'll gather the rest of their things." Her large legs make a familiar *swoosh, swoosh* noise, reminding me how much I will miss hearing her shuffle about.

Anna grabs a doughnut and hugs Abby. When Mrs. Craig sits next to her, Anna raises Abby high and roars like a lion.

I laugh. Since Mrs. Craig didn't hear Ben's story, she doesn't understand Anna's roar, but she laughs with us.

Rachel soon appears, out of breath, in the doorway, holding up two bags of clothes.

"Where's Ben hiding himself?" Mrs. Craig asks, looking around.

"Ben! Come in here and see the girls off," Rachel calls, puttering around the room as if she half expects him to jump out from behind the table or chairs.

"There you are!" She shuffles to the doorway and holds his arm.

I frown, wondering why Rachel is acting so

strangely—and why does Ben take her hand and walk over to us, as if Rachel can't make it on her own?

"So, you're leaving, are you?"

I look up into his brown eyes. They sparkle as usual, but there is a flicker of sadness in them.

"Look what I have here for the each of you." He holds out his free hand—a bear paw, cracked and stained from grease and work.

"Pennies?" I say, trying to hide my disappointment.

"Not just any pennies," he says, letting go of Rachel's hand and giving a penny to each of us. "Lucky pennies. Turn them over."

I squint to see what's on mine. "What is that?"

"A wreath of wheat. Wheat is—what in English do you say for—?" He turns to Rachel and says a word that sounds like *par-noo-silly*.

"Prosperity," offers Rachel.

"Yes. Prosperity! Money can buy many things, it's true. But prosperity grows out of generosity and finding good in ourselves and others."

"So, where did you find these?" I slip my penny in a pocket.

"Where?" Ben gathers us close. "I will tell you the

story of where. When I left Russia many, many years ago to come to America, I was separated from my family and did not know if I would ever see them again."

"Just like us," I murmur.

Ben looks at me. "Yes, just like you and Anna," he says gruffly. "So, I was on one hand happy to go, because I wanted to come to America. But on the other hand, sad—leaving my family behind. You understand about that?"

Anna and I nod.

"It is a long, long way across the ocean to New York, and I will never forget." He pauses, and his eyes get a faraway look in them. "You know how it is when you get carsick, Sara? Well, I was seasick the whole time we crossed the Atlantic—all ten days! The food was horrible, and I lost a lot of weight. You would never know it now by looking at me, eh?" He pats his belly, and a low laugh rolls out of him.

His eyes again glaze over and his voice softens, as if he's in another place and time. "After the boat dropped me and all the other immigrants off at Ellis Island and I had to answer questions and more questions, then suddenly we were free. But who knew what freedom was? I stepped onto the ferry to Manhattan, and, just like you with these little bags, the clothes on my back were the only things I had to my name.

"What I gave you," he says, clasping our hands, "were the first two pennies I earned in America. They were shiny and new back then. Look at the date—nineteen hundred and twenty-three. They are very old, those pennies. Later someone told me pennies are good luck. And for me, maybe that was true.

"I did all right for myself and my family," he adds, winking at Rachel. "Now I am passing on to you something old to take with you on your new journey. Who knows who had those pennies before me? But I took care of them all these years, waiting to give them to someone special."

I finger the penny in my pocket, wondering if there is any luck left in them for me and Anna.

"Thank you, Ben. You too, Rachel. We'll miss you." I give Ben a big hug. For all I know, it's the last time I'll ever see or hug him again. "I'll keep mine forever," I promise, hoping it's a promise I can keep.

It will be like having a part of him with me.

CHAPTER 18

AS WE DRIVE OFF, I HEAR A FAMILIAR SOFT popping noise and look over at Anna. She's pulling her doll apart. She's hardly spoken since the near accident, and there's an absent look to her eyes, as if there's no roar left in her. One by one, I collect the pieces and put her doll back together.

"We have to make one stop," Mrs. Craig says, checking her watch. "I was going to do this later, but I'm running a little late, so we'll take care of it before we go."

I stare out the window, not paying much attention to her chatter. At the corner, a man is selling flowers. Big, long, purple ones.

"Look at those beautiful irises. Should I buy some for the Chandlers? You'll really like Edith and Dan."

Great. Another Dan, another dad.

The flower man walks over to the window, and Mrs. Craig buys two long stems of flowers that are stuck together at the bottom.

"You pay just one," the man tells her, smiling. He has a front tooth missing.

"How nice. Thank you." She hands him a dollar and pulls away from the curb full of flutter. "A twin bulb!" she bubbles. "What a lucky draw!"

I glance at Anna. Like me, she has no clue what Mrs. Craig is talking about.

"Flower bulbs like these are called perennials. They die down in the winter but come back every spring. And sometimes"—she clicks on her turn signal—"they are separated to help them grow." She waits for a car to pass, then makes another turn.

I look at the flowers. "How do you separate them?"

"Well, actually, you just pull them apart. It doesn't hurt the plant. It just makes two plants out of one." She slows and puts her signal on a third time.

I stare out the window at the littered street,

listening to the *click-click-click* of the signal. Fall is here. School will start up soon. I wonder where we'll be—at a new school? In a new house? Will we be home, with Daddy?

As we drive, Mrs. Craig drones on and on. It's the same story I've heard many times before. How nice the new family is. How much they are looking forward to having a sister for their little boy, and that all he wanted for his sixth birthday was a big sister. How his name is Kevin, but everyone calls him Kev, and isn't that cute?

"A sister—?" I start to say, when we turn onto an unfamiliar street. I look over at Anna to see if she's alarmed too, but she has fallen asleep. I look back up at our caseworker.

"Sara," she says in a low, creepy voice that scares me. Anna should be awake and hearing this. Mrs. Craig never whispers. "I know it's hard for you to take care of Anna."

She was right. Anna takes a lot of energy. I glance at my sister looking all peaceful and back at Mrs. Craig.

"Everybody needs a break, now and then. You know, to relax a little and—"

"You mean like Mama," I whisper hotly. "Did she

need a break from us so bad that she had to run away? Maybe they're called breaks because broken things need them."

I look down at my hands, then shoot a side glance at Anna. She doesn't look broken when she's sleeping, but she's definitely broken when she's awake. What about me? Am I broken?

Mrs. Craig keeps talking but my thoughts talk louder. *There's all kinds of broke,* I remind myself.

"Do you see this is the best solution?"

"I guess."

A smile breaks her smooth face into curved lines and dimples. She takes a deep breath and relaxes her shoulders. "I knew you'd understand," she says, turning her wrist to look at her watch.

"Oh no! The time. We need to get a move on."

"If your watch broke, you'd need a break," I tell her, and she laughs, waking up Anna.

"You might be right, there, Sara. My watch is my compass. I have over one hundred cases a week to process, so I'm glued to time."

"One hundred cases of what?"

"Kids needing homes."

Before I can get the image of kids packed into boxes out of my head, she turns into a parking lot.

"Where are we? What is this?"

"We're on the west side of Maple View Center, the residential treatment place I was telling you about, and this is where Anna will live for a while," she says, pulling up to the front door.

"Why just Anna?" I ask, my voice shaking. "Why can't I stay here too?"

Mrs. Craig turns and looks firmly at me. "Sara, we talked about this. It's a special place for Anna." As she talks she punches in a number on her phone.

"You talked, you mean." Two men come out of the front door and walk toward the car.

"Sar—"

"Run, Anna! *Run!*" I shout, before Mrs. Craig can finish her thought. I push Anna out the door. She turns back to the car, crying. "Abby! Abby!"

I toss Abby to her. "Run! They're going to lock you up! Run!" I jump out and rush over to grab my sister's hand, dragging her past the car, but the attendants have already reached us. One of them clamps a hand around my arm, and I fight to get away. The muscle in my arm burns. He tells me not to worry, that everything's going to be okay, but I barely hear him. All I can hear is Anna saying—doing—nothing! The other attendant kneels down and puts an arm around her. She doesn't scream. She doesn't spit. She doesn't bite. What's wrong with her? Of all the times to act normal.

I kick and scream, biting and clawing at the air. "Let me go! Let me go!"

Anna droops like a rag doll—no fight left. She clutches Abby. One arm, I notice, is missing.

"You lied! You lied to us!" I scream at Mrs. Craig. "You said we were going to a new house!"

"Take deep breaths, Sara." Mrs. Craig turns to the attendants. "I'm so sorry. I meant to drop Sara off first, but . . ." She turns to me. "I know this will be hard for a while."

Every word she says feels like a nail being hammered into my skin. Hard? *Hard*?

"Like we talked about in the car, Sara, Anna has to stay here for a while. She needs special care, and the nice people here will give it to her. The Chandlers—"

I start kicking the guy holding me as another

attendant leads Anna away. In a matter of moments, Anna is gone.

When the door closes behind her, something closes inside me, too. "You can't do this! *Help!* Somebody! *Help! Help!*" I shout, but nobody comes running to help.

Mrs. Craig opens the car door for the attendant, who stuffs me into the backseat and belts me in. Then Mrs. Craig hastily walks around to the driver's side.

I fight to get the buckle unbuckled and hear the distinctive *click* as the doors are locked, trapping me in the car.

"You can't do this. You can't hold me against my will. Wasn't that one of the rules in the Foster Youth Bill of Rights they read to us at the Cottages? You can't lock me in a room," I add, looking back at the residential treatment center getting smaller and smaller. When we turn a corner, it disappears altogether.

"You are right, Sara, but there was also the part that says, 'Your foster care provider may impose reasonable restrictions . . . if they determine that any restrictions are necessary to keep order, discipline, or safety. . . .'"

I clench my hands together. "What are they going to

do to her?" I look out the back window, hoping to see Anna running down the street after the car.

"The specialists will test Anna, and she'll eventually be placed in therapeutic foster care. That's like a home for special people." Mrs. Craig stops at a red light and looks back at me, but I stare straight ahead, fuming inside.

"It's green," I almost shout, and she turns back, stepping on the gas. *Special?* "Isn't that what you called jail? Special? There's nothing special about that place." I gulp down tears. "When will I get to see her?" My throat is raw and sore from screaming. *Where is Daddy? Why can't he drive up now and save her?*

"She has to earn your visit, Sara. When she has achieved behavioral goals set for her at the center, they'll allow her to have visitors, but her behavior has to improve before they'll let you see her again."

Achieved behavioral goals? Allowed to have visitors? What is she talking about? By the time we turn the corner and the center disappears, I figure it out. The trap they set has snapped. Anna is caught, and it's all my fault.

"I'll talk with the court, I promise, Sara. I give you my word. You have to trust me on this."

"Give me your word? *Trust you?*"

"You want what's best for your sister, don't you?"

"You lied to us!" I shout, and I cry and cry until no more tears will come. Why am I blaming Mrs. Craig? Wasn't I the one who wished Anna would go away? Of all the trillion and one wishes I made, why is this the one that came true?

Looking down, I spot the missing arm from Anna's doll on the floor of the car. I pick it up and slip it into the side pocket of my duffel bag. Somehow, some way, I will get it to her. My foot hits against something stiff packed inside the duffel bag. I open it. Ben and Rachel had put a photo of me and Anna and them in a frame. I hug it, rocking back and forth.

I'm sorry, Anna. I'm so, so sorry.

Mrs. Craig pulls over to the curb and stops the car. She twists around and looks at me. I'm waiting for her to scold me about telling Anna to run, but she doesn't even mention it.

"Sara, I feel terrible. I didn't want you to have to see that. I have so many kids I am trying to place that sometimes I have to do as much as I can in one trip, but I never meant for you to go through that. Anna was going to have to go to Maple View no matter what. She bites people, Sara. She needs to learn how to deal with her anger and pain in a different way.

"You, on the other hand, need a family. Parents. People who will love you and take good care of you."

Her voice is a distant hum. She sighs and pulls away from the curb. Trees whip past, each one marking a distance that is farther and farther away from my sister and Daddy, and from the hope of ever seeing either of them again.

I touch the lucky penny. There's no luck in it. Maybe I should just throw it out the window. I raise my arm, but something makes my hand stay closed tightly around it.

The drive to my new foster home feels like it takes forever. I want to throw up, but I fight the feeling off.

The car finally slows. I focus on the buildings around us, trying not to think about how I let Daddy down, first by getting us caught, and now by letting them take Anna away. I should have been paying more attention. Hadn't I promised Mama I would watch her? *It won't happen again, I promise, Mama. I'll get her back. You'll see. You can trust me, Mama. I give you my word.*

But in my head, Anna is screaming, *Words get broken!* And she's right.

When Mrs. Craig pulls up to a familiar intersection, I frown. My heart beats faster as she drives through the MacMillans' old neighborhood. I frown even harder when she turns down the street where they'd lived.

"Are the MacMillans still here?" I ask, pressing my face close to the window to search for Sneaker.

"No, they're gone," she answers, pulling into a driveway two doors down from where the MacMillans lived. "Their house is being rented now," she adds.

They should have named the street Foster Kid Row.

CHAPTER 19

"THERE'S OFTEN A SOMEWHAT AWKWARD PERIOD of adjustment," Mrs. Craig explains to Edith Chandler, my new foster mom, as Dan Chandler, my new foster dad, unloads my bag. "Especially with the older ones. They know so much more about what's happening to them."

We stand like planted trees in the front yard. I keep my distance, but I can still hear them.

"Did you—" Mrs. Chandler glances at me and back at Mrs. Craig.

"Yes," Mrs. Craig answers, handing her the flowers. She glances over her shoulder at me and lowers her voice. "She's quite upset."

Quite upset? I didn't get to say good-bye or see inside

the residential center. Does Anna have her own room? Are there other kids in the room with her? What if she wets the bed? Who will hide her sheets?

Questions pile up in my head until I feel like breaking something. I bet it's how Anna feels every time she pulls Abby apart.

I watch Mrs. Craig get into her car, and rest my head against a tree. It feels good to have something to lean against. To me, Daddy is like a tree. Strong. Tall. But in truth, Ben is the real tree.

Daddy is more like a bird, singing his songs, flitting from one place to the next—needing the tree more than the tree needs him. Not that being a bird is a bad thing. It's just harder for birds to stick around.

Why can't people be more like trees?

I glance at the Chandlers' house. It has oatmeal-colored walls with same-colored bricks all around the front. Big windows. I like windows. And it has a big porch all around the front, lined with flowers. Lots of flowers.

Not bad.

The For Rent sign on the MacMillans' house has been taken down. I scan the trees and bushes for a sign of Sneaker. I see a cat sitting under a hedge, but it's not Sneaker.

"Did you know the MacMillans?" I ask, walking over to Mrs. Chandler.

She grins. "Sure, we knew the MacMillans. Not real well. They moved out a couple of days ago, the day before a new family moved in. From what I understand, the new family is leasing the place until the sale is final. They have a girl who looks to be about your age. Maybe you can run down and meet her tomorrow."

I breathe a sigh of relief, secretly glad the MacMillans have moved. After he stole all my stuff, the last person I want to see is Pablo.

"Kev, come meet Sara," Mrs. Chandler calls. A boy runs toward us.

I eye the little runt warily, though I have to admit he's kind of cute.

Kevin looks at me wide-eyed. "Are you going to be my sister? My friend Joey says you're not a real sister. Are you?" His eyes are blue, like mine. He seems big for a six-year-old, but his spiked, sun-bleached hair standing up on end might be why.

"Do I look real?" I ask.

Kevin grins and punches me to test how real I am. "Ow!"

"No punching, Kevin," Mrs. Chandler calls out.

But Kevin seems happy with the results of his test and dances around me. "Wanna see your room?" He stretches out his hand. When I take it, it feels small and sticky and not one bit like Anna's.

"Hang on a sec." I turn to Mr. Chandler. "Do you have the number for the place Anna's in? When can I call my sister?"

"Uh—" Mr. Chandler glances uncomfortably at Mrs. Craig heading for the car and then walks past us, carrying my bag. Mrs. Chandler clears her throat, looking to Mrs. Craig for help.

"Not just yet, Sara," Mrs. Craig says, getting into her car.

"Remember, we talked about that. She needs time. . . ." Her voice fades as she closes her door, gives me one last look, and then waves.

I don't wave back. When her car disappears around the corner, I turn to Kevin. "Is that your cat?" I point to where the cat had been.

Kevin looks where I'm pointing and shakes his

head. "I can't have one. They make Mom sneeze. Those are strays."

Strays? My heart leaps when a couple of kittens peer out from under a bush next door. A quick scan tells me the bad news. None of them is Sneaker.

"Come on in, Sara. Let's get you settled," Mrs. Chandler calls from the porch.

The day is a blur of activity and emotion. Kevin doesn't want to leave me alone, which, in some ways, is annoying. He's always underfoot, and I get a little mad at him for it. But in other ways, he takes my thoughts off Anna, and how scared she must be, and how empty and lost I feel without her.

Kevin has so many things to show me. The dragon costume he's planning to wear for Halloween. Do I want to see it on? Books, books, and more books I can't read. Do I want to read them to him? A race-car set. Do I want to race him? A tool kit. Do I want to build a robot? His new "I Spy" memory game that we play six times in a row before his parents finally rescue me.

"Sara's not a sitter, Kevin. She's a sister. Sitters have no choice but to play with you. Sisters do."

I like that. Having a choice, I mean. I also like my new room. It has pretty yellow wallpaper with tiny green, pink, and purple wildflowers on it. Dark wood around the doors and windows make the room feel warm and safe. Everywhere you look there's wood. Ben would love it here.

Only one thing is missing.

Anna.

CHAPTER 20

I'M UP EARLY THE NEXT MORNING, THOUGH I'M not the first. Plates clank in the kitchen. When I head downstairs, I can hear my foster mom softly singing to herself.

"Oh, you beautiful doll, you great big beautiful doll. Let me put my arms around you. I can never live without you—"

"How do you know that song?" I demand. It's the one Daddy sang to me the night before he never came back.

"Well, g-good morning to you too," Mrs. Chandler answers, frowning slightly. "Let me guess. You don't like that tune?"

"I hate it."

"Then I won't sing it again," she says, drying her hands on a towel. "Did you sleep well?" She carefully folds the towel and sets it on the counter. The sun pours through the window, and I get a good look at her. A twirl of dark curls fall around a thin, pretty face. She's taller than I am, probably the same size as Mama. So what? Mama has a pretty face too. It doesn't mean anything.

"No. I didn't sleep well."

"I'm sorry to hear that." She walks over to me, bends down, and brushes my bangs out of my eyes. "Did you have bad dreams?"

"I don't dream." I pull back.

"Well, we'll just have to fix that, now, won't we?" She draws me into a hug. Her hair smells like strawberries. Anna would have spit on her or bitten her arm.

I pull away and look around, missing Anna so bad. I should never have wished her away. When I wished it, I didn't mean forever. Just for a little while. Long enough for a good family to want us.

"I have to go," I say the minute she releases me.

"Go? Go where?" Her voice pinches to a high note.

"Out." I start for the front door.

"You don't mean outside?" She stands up. "I mean—you haven't even had breakfast yet."

"I'm not hungry." My stomach rumbles loudly at the smell of toast. I breathe in deep and swallow, letting my breath out slowly. Like eating paper towels. It's just another way I fool my stomach into thinking it has been fed. With the smell locked into my memory, I can call on it and bring up the scent anytime I want it to help fill me up.

Toast. Coffee. Daddy. It doesn't matter what I whisper. The scent will always be there.

"You should ask me first b-before just t-taking off," she stammers. "Or at the very least, tell me where you want to go." She twists her hands.

"Daddy Dan" walks in and looks back and forth between us. I take a good look at him, too. He's tall and lean, like Daddy, only his hair is black as a shadow, and his sideburns are silver. His cheeks look like they've been carved in stone. His eyes are warm, brown, and smiling.

Mine aren't. "Where do I want to go?" I answer hotly. "How about to the place where Anna is? They shouldn't have split us up. They said they wouldn't. Grown-ups lie, lie, lie."

Mrs. Chandler wilts. Daddy Dan keeps busy by peeling an orange he's taken from the refrigerator. "Not all grown-ups lie, Sara," he says. Peel. Peel. Peel. "In my line of work, there's an expression, 'Innocent until proven guilty.'"

I stare at him. What more proof does he need? "They lie," I say flatly.

"The story I heard was that Mrs. Craig said she might have let you go in with Anna, but—"

"We ran away. That was then. But that doesn't give her the right to break her promise. She said we would stay together." I squirm, anxious to leave. "You could have taken both of us." I glare at them, wondering what the excuse will be this time.

To my surprise, Mrs. Chandler starts to cry. Daddy Dan goes over to her and hugs her, but when he looks back at me, the look in his eyes is disappointment.

So what if my words hurt? Lies hurt too. Mrs. Craig should never have lied. It grows so quiet, I can hear the clock ticking in the living room down the hall.

Mr. Chandler breaks the silence. "She needs help, Sara. Anna needs—"

"I've heard all about what Anna needs, but everybody's wrong. Anna needs *me*." I feel tears pricking my eyes.

He holds out a section of orange. I hesitate, then snatch it from his hand.

"You can go to the end of the block and back," he says, opening the door. "We'll wait to eat breakfast until after you get home."

Home. I squeeze past him. They think this is home? My real home is on Elm Street or with the Silvermans. Not here.

"Whatever," I say, banging the door behind me. I need air, not arguments.

"Let her go," I hear him say through the door. "She misses her sister. It's going to take time."

When I look back, I see them hug and feel a tug. Not a steal-something kind of tug. Worse. A this-hurts tug. It should be my real Mama and Daddy I watch, hugging each other. But the way Mama and Daddy got close wasn't with hugs. The way they got close was with words. Hurtful words. The very thing that ripped them apart.

I don't need them. I don't need anyone.

CHAPTER 21

A COUPLE OF DOORS DOWN I SPOT A RED-HAIRED girl setting up a table, putting pitchers and cups on it. I slow my pace. Now what? Meet the new neighbor girl Mrs. Chandler talked about? A sign above the stand says something I can't read, but the number on it says 50¢.

A boy who looks like he might be her brother—same reddish hair—pokes up from under the table and plops some cups down.

"Hiya!" the girl yells, running over to me with sandals on her hands instead of her feet. "You must be the new girl we heard about. I'm Lexie. We're new too. We just moved here. What's your name?"

I stop and stare.

"Want a Tropical Thirst Quencher?" she says before I can answer. Not that I was going to.

"Juice," she says, pointing to the pitcher. "It's fifty cents, but for you, we'll call it a quarter."

"I'm not thirsty," I lie, fingering the penny in my pocket. Really, though, my throat is so dry that I can hardly swallow.

Lexie shrugs. "You can have a cup for free if you want."

I barely taste the juice going down.

"This is my brother, Skeeter." She sees my face and it's like she reads my mind or something. "He likes bugs," she explains.

"Oh."

Skeeter turns as red as his hair.

"So, what's your name?" Lexie asks again.

"Samantha," I blurt. It just kind of pops out.

"Samantha! Omigosh. Really? What a kawinkeedink. Did you hear that, Skeeter? Her name is Samantha. My best friend's name is Samantha!"

Kawinkeedink? What kind of a word is that?

"Best friend? That's nice." I look behind her, wondering what having a best friend would be like. My eyes catch something moving in the bushes. Sneaker?

"We moved here from Riverside. It's this city in Southern California. I wish Samantha were really here. Not you. I mean, don't be hurt or anything, but I was talking about the other Samantha, my best friend."

And I wish Anna were here, I think but don't say. "Got any cats around?"

"Ta-ha!" It's a strange little laugh. "Dozens! Strays all over the place."

Someone pulls up in a car, pays fifty cents, and buys some juice. "Back in a sec," Lexie calls over her shoulder. I thought she was talking to the people in the car, but when they drive away, I realize she was talking to me.

When she leaves, Skeeter and I look everywhere but at each other, fishing for something to talk about. He has freckles the size of small pebbles all over his arms and face.

He stares down at one of his shoes like it might run off, then darts another look at me. "You like bugs?"

It seems like a strange question, but I nod.

"Me too. I just found a treehopper!"

"I used to live here," I blurt, not having a clue what a treehopper is.

"Here? You mean in Oakview?"

"No. Here in your house." I watch a look of amazement slide over his face.

Lexie comes out carrying another pitcher of juice. Skeeter runs over to her. "You're not going to believe this, Lex. She—" He looks at me, frowning. "What did you say your name was again?"

"Sara—mantha," I say, almost forgetting myself.

"Saramantha used to live here! In our house!"

Lexie stares at me, finally speechless. "You used to live in our house?" A strange look passes between them.

"The stinky sheets!" they cry in unison.

"They aren't mine!" The words tumble out as heat rushes to my face. "They're my sister's." I catch myself too late.

"You have a sister? How old?" Lexie asks, perking up.

"Twelve," I mumble. Some holes are hard to crawl out of.

"Twelve years old and she wets the bed?"

"Leave her alone!" I yell. "She can't help it."

Lexie and Skeeter exchange looks. "Wait here," they order, running toward their house, hollering, "Mom, Mom!" like the place is on fire.

Yeah, right. Hang around for them to say mean things about me and my sister? I don't think so. I have a cat to look for.

When the door closes behind them, I turn toward my new house and, to my surprise, a small black-and-white cat pounces out and grabs at my shoe.

"Sneaker!" I scoop her up and hold her close. "It's you. It's really you! You're alive. You're okay!"

I press my face into her soft coat. "Let's get outta here so I can tell you about Anna—it's so sad, Sneak." She purrs against my chest, smelling like cat food.

Before I get ten steps away, footsteps thunder down the porch stairs behind me. I don't turn around.

"Hey, where'd she go?" Skeeter calls.

"There she is." Lexie sees me before I can duck behind a tree. "Samantha! Wait! We have something for you! Hey. What's she holding? Stop her, Skeet! She's got Poof!"

Lexie sprints across the grass with Skeeter at her heels. They catch up to me at the neighbor's house. Lexie grabs for Sneaker, but I hold on tight.

"Give me back my cat!" she shouts.

I twist away and hug Sneaker even tighter. Skeeter

"Poofy? What kind of a dumb name is that? Look, her name is not Poof, Poofy, or any other dumb name you come up with. Her name is Sneaker. I found her when I lived here. Only, the foster parents I was staying with said that they were going to take her to the animal shelter and have her put to sleep!"

Okay, so I kind of made up that last part, but I'm mad.

Lexie gasps. "Put to sleep?" For a moment, she almost looks understanding. "That's awful! Who'd do that?" Then, quick as a snap, she turns mean again. "Look, the cat is mine, and I want her back. What's with you? Stealing other people's pets!"

"I didn't steal anything. I told you, I'm just taking back what's mine."

"Does your sister steal too?"

I could have spit at her. How dare she say stuff about Anna? Then Kevin shows up dressed like a dragon.

"Leave my new sister alone!" he shouts. He stares out of the mouth of the dragon, even though the dragon's eyes are on top of his head. "I know karate," he adds, doubling up his small fists.

"New sister?" Lexie frowns.

"We're Sara's new foster family!" Kevin shouts. I sling one arm around him and hold Sneaker in the other.

"Sara?" Lexie glares at me. "I thought you said your name is Samantha! You steal *and* lie?" she explodes. "What else? Do you cheat, too? I don't think people who lie, steal, and cheat should be allowed near our cat, do you, Skeet?" She turns to her brother for support.

Skeeter shrugs and looks over our heads like he's watching for something to fall from the sky.

I stay as still and silent as a rock. Ben Silverman told me once that when people are being bullies, sometimes silence is the best defense.

"Sara's sister didn't get to stay with us. Sara doesn't know if she'll ever see her again!" Kevin shouts. "So quit being so mean."

Kevin's words stab at me, but Lexie stands her ground.

"It's too bad all that stuff happened to you. But I found this cat, and I've been taking care of her. She's mine. You're the one who left her behind, not me."

"I didn't leave her!" I say hotly. "Mrs. Craig told us 'No pets' when she took us back to the Silvermans'."

"Yeah, well, I have no clue who any of those people are, but Poof is mine!" Lexie says stiffly.

"'Fraid not," I say just as stiffly, though it's hard to stand up to someone who is taller than you and really loud.

"Skeeter, tell her whose cat this is!" Lexie spins around to face her brother.

"That's not fair!" I shout. "You can't ask him. Of course he'll say Sneaker's yours. He's your brother!"

"I'm *your* brother!" Kevin's face lights up. "I'll be on your side, Sara! It'll be a tie!"

"Maybe we should let the cat decide," Skeeter says.

We all stare at him. What does he mean, let the cat decide? How?

"Hand me the cat. You walk twelve steps this way, and you twelve steps that way, and then I'll put down the cat, and we'll see who she goes to."

Lexie looks smug and grins at Skeeter. "Good idea, Skeet. Put her down, cat burglar," she adds, planting herself beside her brother.

I start to worry. Will Sneaker remember me when it really counts?

"Can we bend down and reach for her?" I ask,

staying just as close to Skeeter's other side as Lexie is on her side.

Skeeter shakes his head. "Why do girls have to make such a big deal out of everything? Just stand over there and see who the cat goes to!" He glares at his sister and lowers his voice, probably thinking I can't hear him. But I do.

"You hardly pay any attention to that cat, Lexie. What difference does it make who has her?"

Lexie's mouth drops open, and then she closes it so tight, it's just a thin, angry line. "Can it, Skeeter."

Skeeter ignores her and reaches toward me. Reluctantly, I hand him the cat. At Skeeter's count, Lexie and I each take twelve steps to either side of him and turn around.

"Close your eyes," Skeeter commands.

"What?" Lexie glares at him.

"Close your eyes. I'm putting her down. No signaling. No coaxing. No nothing. Just close your eyes and we'll see who she goes to."

"Pick Sara! Pick Sara!" Kevin shouts, clapping his hands.

"No picking sides," Skeeter tells him.

I close my eyes. *Please pick me. Please!* It seems like forever before I can't stand it anymore and open my eyes. I can see Lexie has opened hers, too, because she's looking all over the place.

"Looks like nobody won," Skeeter announces, motioning toward the porch. Sneaker is busy drinking water.

"I still say she's mine," I say, disappointed that Sneaker didn't choose me, but nobody's listening.

Instead, Skeeter and Lexie pull open the box they'd brought from the house before the big chase.

Skeeter lifts something out of the box.

"Cowwy!" I shout. "But how—"

"Mom found it mixed up in the stinky—in the sheets," he explains.

Suddenly, it all starts to make sense. In our hurry to pull up Anna's sheets, we must have scooped up Cowwy, Mama's letter, and the picture and stuffed them all in the box together. I probably caught my finger on the necklace when putting the sheets in the box.

"You didn't also find a jacket, did you, and an envelope with a picture in it?"

"Yep. They're in here too," Skeeter answers.

I grab the jacket out of the box and wrap it around me, happy to have it back. The envelope is a new one, and it's been sealed closed. I slip it into the front pocket of the jacket.

The moment would have been the best ever, if I didn't think of one awful thing: Pablo didn't steal anything. "The mirror in the box," I groan.

Skeeter frowns. "There wasn't a mirror in the box."

I don't say a word. They don't have to know I blamed Pablo for stealing stuff he never took. He wasn't the thief—I was. I took his rainmaker. That's why he gave me the mirror and said all that stuff about mirrors reflecting who we are. He meant me, the thief. He knew, and now he's gone and there's no way to tell him I'm sorry.

"Kevin! Sara!" Mrs. Chandler waves from the door. "Time for breakfast."

"Coming, Mom!" Kevin shouts.

"I'm getting Sneaker," I announce.

To my surprise, Skeeter steps between me and the porch. "I think it's choice time," he says.

I frown. "Choice time?"

"The stuff you left behind, or the cat."

"Take the cat, Sara!" Kevin shouts, jumping up and down. "The cat, the cat!"

But Kevin doesn't know that all I have left of my family is in the box.

"So, which is it?" Lexie asks. Her eyes are almost laughing. If I were Anna, I'd bite her.

"The stuff," I hiss. I grab Kevin's hand. "Come on, Kev. Let's go home."

"She's a mean girl," Kevin says as we walk back to the Chandlers'.

I look over my shoulder just as Lexie takes Sneaker into her house. Skeeter's still in the yard staring after us.

"Ben Silverman, our last foster parent, once told me that people can get mean when something they love is taken away from them," I answer, slowly climbing the porch steps.

"Are you going to be mean because they took your sister away?" He twists his neck to look up at me.

"I don't know," I answer. "Sometimes mean just happens."

That night, after Mr. and Mrs. Chandler finish tucking Kevin in and saying their good nights to me, I lie alone in bed, staring at the ceiling. Cowwy is tucked tight under my arm. When I turn my head, I try to pretend Anna's there. I can almost see her green eyes, but after a while all I see is the dark, empty space.

Reaching across what would have been her side of the bed, I grab the blanket and make a long divider down the middle with it. When I'm done, I flip over so that my back is pressed against the bundle of blanket, and some of the sad feelings start to slip away. It's easier to picture Anna here when I'm not trying to see her, when I just pretend that the bundle of blanket is her back pressed against mine.

It's what helps me finally fall asleep.

CHAPTER 23

WHEN I WAKE UP, BIRDS ARE SINGING OUTSIDE my window. They make me think of Daddy. I overheard Mrs. Craig saying that Daddy was a jailbird now. I picture him in his big cage, trying to get out, and even though the sun is flooding into my room, I get all sad for him.

Out in the hallway, Kevin races downstairs, pounding his feet with each step.

"Shhh, you'll wake up Sara," I hear Mrs. Chandler say. But she's wrong. I'm already awake.

"Get your things together, Kevin. Dad's taking you over to Andy's on his way to work."

"Can Sara come?"

"Not this time. We have an appointment."

"What's a pointment?" I hear Kevin ask.

"An appointment is a time set aside to see someone."

My heart thumps hard. She's taking me to see Anna! I just know it! I leap from bed and quickly throw on some clothes, and then I race to the bathroom to brush my teeth.

When I arrive in the kitchen, Mrs. Chandler looks at me, starts to say something, but then stops herself.

"What?"

"Aren't those the same shorts and T-shirt you had on yesterday?"

I look down and back up at her. "I think so." What is this? A memory test?

"Sara, you have a whole closetful of clothes that we bought for you. Did you try on any of them?"

"These work fine," I answer, reaching for an apple and anxious to hear all about seeing Anna. I'll wait for her to tell me so she doesn't think I was eavesdropping.

Midway between me and the apple, she gently catches my arm and wraps a hand around my wrist. "Did you wash your hands this morning after going to the bathroom?"

I jerk my hand away. "Yes," I lie. I really want that apple.

To my shock, she takes my hand and lifts it to her nose. "I don't smell any soap on it."

Again I jerk my hand away. I'm not used to people smelling my hands.

"Why don't you wash them again in the sink, and then you can help yourself to some fruit," she says, pointing to the sink.

"I know where the sink is," I tell her, running the water over my hands and then squeezing on the soap.

"The apples are already washed," she adds, handing one to me.

"You wash apples?" I reach past for another, redder one, and she puts back the one she was holding.

"Yes. I do. They could have pesticides on them," she explains. "Pesticides kill bugs, but they can harm people, too, if we don't wash off the fruit and vegetables. Cereal?" she adds.

I stare at the bowl of cornflakes. "Did you wash these, too?" The flakes look a little damp.

"No, but I poured some milk on for you. Want some?"

"Yeah. Sure."

"Yes, please," she says.

"You want some too?" I grab a second bowl.

"I meant that you should say, 'Yes, please,'" she answers.

I sigh. Living with the Chandlers sure comes with a lot of rules. Wash hands. Say please. What next?

Mr. Chandler comes in wearing a big smile. "Good morning, Sara! So, how did you sleep last night?"

"I would have slept a lot better if Anna was here," I answer. He glances over at Mrs. Chandler, but they do that a lot—look at each other after I say something.

"Did you have sweet dreams?" he presses.

"I don't dream," I tell him.

"Well, hopefully that will change someday soon. Sweet dreams are a real treat."

"Like ice cream," Kevin says, hoisting his backpack over his shoulders. "With chocolate sauce," he adds.

Mr. Chandler smiles at him and looks back at me. "Can I give you a hug good-bye?"

I hesitate and don't stand up. "Why? It's not like you're not coming back," I add. Maybe I would have hugged him if he'd kept Anna, too.

He gives Mrs. Chandler another quick look, and then he looks back at me and smiles again. "You don't have to hug us, Sara. I was just asking."

I narrow my eyes. Last time I gave Daddy a hug good-bye, he never came back. I'm starting to kind of like Mr. Chandler, so I decide that hugging him is definitely not a good idea.

"No hug," I say, turning back to my cereal. I don't even have to look at him to know that he has looked again at Mrs. Chandler.

"The good thing about hugs is that they can be saved for later. Have a great day, you two." He walks over and kisses Mrs. Chandler. I don't see it, but I hear the little smack and see them hugging each other out of the corner of my eye. Seeing them makes me feel both good and bad inside. Good for them that they have each other to hug, but bad for me since my hugs have run away, been sent to jail, or are locked up in a residential treatment center.

After Mr. Chandler and Kevin are gone, Mrs. Chandler explains what the day is going to look like. "We have someone we'd like you to go see," she says, making my heart pump hard again.

The excitement builds in me, and it's all I can do

not to shout, *I know!* Finally, I can't stand it anymore. "It's Anna, right?" I ask, hoping she'll say yes, but the smile melts off my face when she shakes her head.

"I'm taking you to see a doctor. She's a counselor, Sara. Her name is Dr. Mira Kitanovski. She's from Yugoslavia."

"You-go-who?" I ask, crushed that we aren't going to see Anna. Who wants to go see a doctor? I'm not even sick.

"Yugoslavia. It's a country across the ocean. It's not called Yugoslavia anymore. There was a war—try not to talk with food in your mouth, sweetie."

Well, that's going to be hard. She's talking to me, and I'm eating. How else do I talk except with food in my mouth?

"Swallow first," she says, like she hears my thought. "I want to prepare you. Dr. Kitanovski has a heavy accent, so she might be hard to understand at first, but I think you're really going to like her."

"Why does she want to talk to me?" I feel like my blood is draining out of my head and arms and fingers. It's like a warning to watch out, or something bad's going to happen.

"She talks to kids and makes them feel better," Mrs. Chandler explains.

"I feel fine," I answer, before remembering not to talk with food in my mouth. A cornflake flies out and lands on the table.

"That's why we don't talk with food in our mouth," she says, wiping it up with a napkin. "She'll show you pictures, and you can tell stories about them."

I look at her and down at my empty bowl. Is this meeting a trap to prove that I don't know how to read? Or is it another kind of center, and they're taking me there to lock *me* up this time? I study her face for some sign that she's hiding something, but her face looks normal.

"Did you want to put on something fresh before we leave?" she asks.

I frown and look again at what I'm wearing. "No. This is good."

"Okay, then. Let's go visit Dr. Kitanovski." She sticks the dirty dishes in the dishwasher and follows me out the door. I crawl into the backseat, picturing Anna sitting next to me, and I wait for her to start the car.

"Buckle up. 'Click it or ticket,'" she says, smiling

when she sees me frown. "It's a slogan the police are saying to get people to put on their seat belts."

I'm not sure what a slogan is, but I buckle up anyway.

When we pull out of the driveway, I see Lexie playing with Sneaker, and I stiffen. Mrs. Chandler looks at me in the rearview mirror and follows my gaze.

"I'm really sorry about the cat situation," she says hastily. "When I'm around them, I can't breathe. I'm not trying to be mean. It's just something I can't help."

I don't say anything. After a while she turns on the radio and hums to different tunes. The music makes me think of Daddy, and I start wondering what he's doing.

And Mama—where's she?

When I next look up, we're downtown, and all the shops are open. I stare at the people, wondering where they're going and what they're buying. Shops soon turn to houses.

"Are we almost there?" I shift uncomfortably in my seat.

"Pretty close."

After about fifteen more minutes of driving, we finally pull into a crowded parking lot and find a space right up close to the door.

"I called ahead and reserved a spot," Mrs. Chandler says, turning off the engine and smiling.

I make my lips go into a smile, but inside, nothing seems funny.

Mrs. Chandler takes a deep breath before opening her door. "Sometimes having a third person to talk to who isn't a family member helps to—" She stops to search for a word.

"To get my sister back?" I ask hopefully, and Mrs. Chandler looks away, giving me my answer.

"What I'm trying to say is that whatever you say to her is between you and her, Sara. You don't have to worry about her telling anyone your answers."

"What answers? I thought I was telling stories?"

"You are, sort of. She'll show you some pictures, and you tell her what you think is happening in them."

I get out of the car and stare at the big white building. It's a funny game they want me to play, but whatever makes them happy, I guess.

"Words and pictures, or just pictures?" I ask, testing again to see if it's a trap.

"Just pictures."

I sigh a big sigh of relief, and Mrs. Chandler smiles.

"You'll do just fine. There's nothing to worry about."

I hesitate at the door. "This isn't a trick, is it? To get me to go in, and then you'll lock the door behind me?"

To my surprise, her eyes tear up. "No, Sara. It's not a trick. Dan and I won't trick you. Ever."

Her face looks like she's telling the truth, but so did Mrs. Craig's when she said that Anna and I would never be split up, so I look around very carefully when we walk through the door. The office is small, with fancy red chairs that have curved legs.

The wallpaper is made to look like a wooded path, and I swear it looks like I could just up and walk right through the wall.

I try to picture where the path leads. Maybe it's like the path Little Red Riding Hood took when she got into trouble with the wolf.

A glass window slides open, and a head pokes out.

"Sara?" Another woman walks out a door leading into the glassed-in area, and she smiles at me. I tense up. "You must be Sara." She walks over and bends down, putting her hand out for me to shake. I look at it, wondering if she has washed it. When it's close to mine, I grab it and pull it to my nose.

Her hand smells like soap. I let go and then re-grab it, this time to shake it.

Mrs. Chandler laughs uncomfortably. "Sorry about that. We had a lesson earlier on washing our hands."

"No problem. I'm glad I passed the test," the uniformed lady answers, smiling.

"Ready to go back and see the doctor?" She guides me through the door and down a short hallway.

"Ah, you must be Sara," a rich, deep voice says. The person attached to the voice is round, with puffy cheeks and wire-gray hair pulled up into a bun on top of her head. She is wearing a big yellow tent-dress that matches the walls and swishes when she walks. "I am Dr. Kitanovski," she says, talking very slowly, like I might not get it the first time. "I am sorry for my talking. Can you understand what I am saying?" Only when she says it, it sounds like *"vat I am say ink."*

I grin. She's a lot like Rachel Silverman. I like her. "Yeah, I understand," I answer, and she smiles. Her office is filled with books. They're on an old claw-legged table in one corner, on her desk, on the floor, in bookcases lining the walls. Red ones, yellow ones, blue ones, white ones, green ones, black ones, and orange;

sitting-down ones, standing-up ones, open ones, closed ones. The air smells of them, and something sweet. Maybe the sweet smell is her.

"This is good," she says, only when she says it, it sounds more like *"Zeese is goot."*

"You like pictures, yes?"

I nod as she pulls a stack of pictures out of a box on her desk.

She smiles warmly and sits me in a comfy chair that hugs me when I sit. It's by a small, round table that has a lamp on it. The lamp is full of liquid, and purple bubbles float up and down.

"I show you a picture and you tell a story you see, yes?"

Again I nod, but when she holds up the picture, it's a picture of three pebbles. Only one of the pebbles is white.

"What you make of this picture. You like it?" Her face crinkles up with worry lines.

"It's nice," I lie, looking away. Even I know that lying to make someone feel better is still a lie.

"What in it do you see, Sara? Look close."

I stare at the three pebbles, turning it this way and

that. "Well, it's three stones that are different shapes and colors. One of them is all white."

"These stones, they have a story, yes?"

"Kind of. They are together in your picture, but they didn't come from the same place."

"No? What place they come?"

"This one," I say, pointing to the speckled one, "probably broke off of a mountain. This one"—I point to the reddish one—"probably came from underground somewhere, and this one"—I point to the white one—"came from a stream. All the color got washed off and the water polished it up."

"Very good, Sara." She put the picture back on her desk and opened a drawer, pulling out three stones, just like the ones in the picture.

"You have the stones!"

"Yes. I have a story, too. Want to hear?"

I grin. Dr. Knows-Something-or-Other is reminding me of Ben, and I love Ben's stories.

"I say this stone"—she pushes the speckled one toward me—"is how you see you."

"And this stone"—she nudges the red one so it rests beside the speckled one—"is how others see you."

"*Okaaaay,*" I say, drawing out the "ay," because I'm not sure her story is as good as Ben's after all.

"And this white one, what do you think that might be?"

I review in my mind what she has told me. The first one is how I see myself. The second one is how others see me, so what's left? I squirm, fingering Ben's penny in my pocket. Ben would know the answer. What would he say the other one means?

"I don't know," I finally admit.

"No worries," she says, saying "worries" like it starts with a *v*.

"What about this one, what picture do you see?"

She holds up another picture of a slender woman, stretching her arms high.

"A dancer," I say quickly. The game is getting easier with each picture.

"Do you like to dance?" she asks, and I shrug. Anna and I liked dancing with the leaves, but I don't think that's the dancing she means. Pablo's box comes to mind, with the tiny dancer twirling in front of the mirror in the box he gave me.

"I like music," I answer. "I sing like Daddy."

"You sing!" Her eyes widen and a smile spreads

across her face. "Can you sing something for me?" The word "something" comes out *"somesing."*

While she gets comfortable in her chair, I sing Daddy's song "Old Tears," and her eyes bulge like frogs' eyes and turn wet and glassy before I'm done.

"You are a beautiful singer, Sara. I feel your song here." She pats her heart. "These old tears you sing of. Who are they for?"

My throat tightens. Mama pops up in my mind, followed by Daddy.

"My sister," I finally whisper.

She bends down and looks up into my face. "You miss her, yes?"

I nod.

"And you worry about her?"

I keep nodding.

"What if I try to check on her and let you know how she is doing—would that make you feel better?"

"You'll do that? You'll check to make sure she's okay?" I jump up and hug her.

"There, there," she says, and pats my back.

After a little bit, she smiles and takes another picture off the pile. "And this picture? What do you see here?"

I stare long and hard at the next picture. "A witch flying away on a cloud broom," I finally answer, handing it back to her.

"Show me this witch you see," she says, taking my hand and guiding it to the picture.

I point out the witch and the broom.

"This witch, where is she flying to?"

I stare at the dark, witch-shaped stain and look away. Except for the pointy hat, it could be Mama flying away, but I don't want to say that, so I shrug. "I don't know," I mumble.

She props the picture up on the table beside her. "Who's flying away from Sara?" she asks, staring at the picture, and before I can stop them, tears prick my eyes, stinging them. I try to blink them away, but they spill down my cheeks and drip onto my lap.

Dr. Kitanovski hugs me and says soothing things that I can't understand because she's not speaking in English anymore. "You come back and see me, yes?" she finally says.

I shrug but then nod, not wanting to hurt her feelings. "Do we have to look at more pictures?" I ask, hoping she'll say no.

"Next time, we play games. You like games?"

I shrug again. "I don't know too many, but I can learn."

She hugs me again. "Yes. You can learn. You can teach me things, too," she adds, and I nod, even though I don't know a thing I can teach her.

"This is for you," she says, giving me a piece of paper with a squiggly line on it. "Draw a picture for me for next time, and use that line in your picture. You can do that?"

I look at the S-shaped line and nod. "Okay. I'll draw you a picture." Of what, I wasn't sure, but maybe I'd think of something between now and then, whenever that will be.

"And don't forget the white stone," she reminds me. "Think of what story it might be trying to tell."

CHAPTER 24

"IT LOOKS LIKE YOU AND THE DOCTOR HAD FUN, Sara," Mrs. Chandler says on the way home. "Did you like her?"

I nod. "She doesn't tell stories too good," I admit, "but she likes to play games. We're going to play some of them next time I see her."

"Sounds fun! Maybe you can teach me some, and we can play them together during the week."

I don't answer and she doesn't push.

"Lexie came over while you were getting dressed."

"What did she want?" I snap.

"She says she's sorry," Mrs. Chandler says, turning onto our street. "Something about making you choose. Anyway, she wants to see if you and she can be friends."

"I don't need a friend. I need Anna!" I shout, wadding up the paper Dr. Kitanovski gave me to draw on and throwing it onto the floor of the car.

Mrs. Chandler pulls into the driveway and turns off the engine. "Can you at least talk to her?"

I start to say no, when a movement in the window catches my eye. I turn, only to see Lexie's face staring right at me. I cry out, startled, and they both start laughing.

"It's not funny!" I shout.

"We're not laughing at you," Mrs. Chandler says, still laughing. "It's just funny when someone presses her face against a window."

"Not to me." I stare straight ahead, refusing to look at Lexie, but out of the corner of my eye I try to see if she's got Sneaker with her.

"I'm sorry I was so mean," Lexie says through the window.

"Sara—" Mrs. Chandler starts to say, then stops. "I have snacks inside, if you girls are hungry."

With all the growling my stomach does, I can't

hide that I'm always hungry, but does *she* have to eat with us?

"Thank you, Mrs. Chandler. That sounds great," Lexie says. She sounds really nice now.

They head up the porch steps, but I stay in the car, staring out the front window.

"Are you coming, Sara?" Mrs. Chandler calls over her shoulder. I know she sees me. *Does it look like I'm coming?*

They disappear inside the house, which is fine with me. I bend over and pick up the wadded-up paper from Dr. Kitanovski and uncrinkle it. When I smooth it out on my lap, I smile, because it looks just as wrinkly as Dr. Kitanovski. I search for a pencil and find one on the floor, along with a Life Saver. It has a little fuzz on it, but I eat it anyway. Cherry, my favorite.

I stare at the S and turn the paper on its side. Then I see it. The S is the rim on Daddy's hat. I draw it the best I can remember.

When I'm done, I look out the window to see if Sneaker's anywhere around. She isn't, but other strays leap in and out of the bushes. I count them and stop after twelve.

A car is creepy when you're the only one sitting in it, so I get out and slam the door to let them know I'm coming.

When I get inside, I see Lexie and Mrs. Chandler at the table, heads together, laughing. Lexie is making faces with the fruit on her plate.

"The cantaloupe can be the smile," she says, putting her slice down at the bottom of her plate.

I would have turned my slice upside down.

"Or a frown, if you want," she quickly adds, looking over her shoulder at me.

"Grapes make good eyes if you poke a raisin through the top." She pokes raisins into two grapes and slices off the bottoms so they'll stand up. "Banana slices make good noses." She polishes off her face and shows it to Mrs. Chandler. Even though she doesn't show it to me, I can see it. I hate to say it, but making food faces looks fun.

"You want to try one, Sara?" Mrs. Chandler asks, sliding a can of pineapple toward me.

I want to, but I don't want to. I feel the pull inside me. "Not really," I answer, edging toward the table. "But if you're going to make me, I guess I could try one."

For the next half hour or so, we make funny faces with pineapple slices, cherries, orange peels, and any other thing we can get our hands on. I even make hair out of stick pretzels for one of my faces. Each face makes us laugh louder and harder. Then we eat them.

The phone rings, and I jump up. Maybe it's Mrs. Craig calling to say I can talk to Anna. I closely watch Mrs. Chandler's face when she answers it.

"She's right here," she says, and my heart takes wing. "Do you want to talk to her?"

I jump up from the table, but it isn't me she hands the phone to, it's Lexie.

"Sorry, sweetie. It's Mrs. Anderson," Mrs. Chandler says as she sits back down at the table.

I sink against the back of my chair and push the plate with my half-eaten funny faces away.

Lexie cups her hand over the phone. "Can you come over tomorrow?" she asks me before hanging up.

I look at Mrs. Chandler, who nods. "It's fine with me, Sara. Do you want to go to Lexie's tomorrow?"

I miss Sneaker, so I nod. "I guess."

"She said yes, Mom," Lexie practically shouts into the phone. "Okay, I'm on my way. Bye. Love you too."

"Miss Penny's cat had more kittens," Lexie says to us after she hangs up the phone. "Mom says they're all coming into our yard, searching for food."

"Who's Miss Penny?" I ask.

"She lives in the house on the other side of us. She won't fix her cat, and so it keeps having kittens. This is her cat's third litter."

"Someone should call Animal Control. They'd get her to get that cat fixed," Mrs. Chandler says while wrapping up the leftover fruit.

"Dad says they'll become fielders and keep the mouse population down," Lexie adds.

"Not too many fields left around here," Mrs. Chandler says, wiping the table. "Not that I'm against mouse control! Still, it's cats that are overrunning the neighborhood these days, not mice."

"It's a catastrophe," Lexie says, and they both start laughing.

I don't get what's so funny, so I just sit there.

"What's a cat's trophy?" I ask when Mrs. Chandler comes back into the kitchen.

She frowns slightly, then smiles. "A catastrophe? A catastrophe is a disaster," she answers.

I know all about disasters. Mama taking off. Disaster. Daddy getting put in jail. Disaster. Anna being taken to the special center. Disaster. And none of it is funny, so why were they laughing?

"Lexie was using a play on words," Mrs. Chandler explains, brushing my hair away from my face. "Catastrophe is spelled C-A-T-A-S-T-R-O-P-H-E. Since it starts with the word 'cat,' it's a funny play on words." She looks at me, eyebrows raised, like she's asking if I understand, so I nod.

"You really like Lexie, don't you?" I ask, emphasizing Lexie's name.

Mrs. Chandler smiles. "Yes, I do like Lexie. She's got a lot of spirit."

"What about me? Do I have spirit?"

"You have a lot of spirit, Sara."

I feel better knowing she likes me, too.

"I have to start on dinner. Want to help?" She waits for me to answer.

"Sure!"

"Be sure to wash your hands before we start."

Mrs. Chandler has a thing about washing hands. "Okay," I say on my way to the bathroom. "Then I'll sing you a song."

"By heart?"

"No, with my mouth," I shout over the running water, and shake my head at the thought. Who sings a song from their heart?

CHAPTER 25

I HIDE MAMA'S LETTER IN A BOX STASHED IN MY closet, along with other treasures I find around the neighborhood. Rocks. Feathers. Strings. Buttons. Then, every night before going to sleep, I grab Mama's letter, try to sound out some words, and then put it back in the box to keep it safe.

There's not a day or night that I don't look at it. And not a day or night passes that I don't worry about Anna. And barely a moment passes that I'm not glued to the radio, listening for Daddy's songs.

"I never thought I'd be a fan of country music," Mr. Chandler says one morning, slipping in behind me and reaching to turn the volume down on the radio. "But I can see why you like it, Sara."

"Daddy can make his guitar sound like someone singing," I tell him. "You don't even need words to know what it says. Bet you can't play guitar." I look at him closely, but his face doesn't give anything away.

"Nope. Can't play guitar. Can't sing. Have two left feet when it comes to dancing, but I can juggle. Does that count?"

"I guess." I never saw anyone juggle before.

He smiles and picks up a glass apple from Mrs. Chandler's fake-fruit bowl, and looks around for two more things to juggle.

"I wouldn't be tossing Mrs. Chandler's apple in the air," I warn, looking to see if she's around. She isn't. "It'll break if you drop it, and Mrs. Chandler seems pretty attached to it. She was dusting it earlier and looking at it like she'd never seen an apple before."

He reaches down and picks up a couple of Kevin's rubber balls from a box on the chair.

"She is attached to it," he agrees, and just like that he starts to juggle the apple with the two rubber balls.

"Don't worry. I'll be careful. Know what I learned about juggling?" he asks. His voice jiggles when he talks.

"That you shouldn't talk while throwing a glass ball in the air?" I answer.

He laughs, never missing a beat or a ball. The balls make a soft *ffftt-ffftt* sound as they hit his hands. The glass apple makes a higher, more breakable sound.

"I learned that life is like juggling."

Yeah. Juggling from one house to another, I think but don't say.

"I learned that to juggle work and money"—I gasp as he catches the glass apple in the bend of his elbow while still juggling the two remaining balls—"takes a good head and a keen eye for detail, but family—"

I suck in air and hold my breath, throwing my hands to my ears and pressing hard against them. He flips the apple in the air and catches it, holding it up in one hand while juggling the two rubber balls with the other. I let go of my ears.

"Family is like glass," he says, never taking his eye off the apple. "A family is strong, but fragile. Something to protect and defend. Something to care for and take care of."

He catches all the balls and slowly puts the glass one back in the bowl, and then he leans down to look at me. "In this family, every member takes really good care of the others. And that includes how we feel about you. We think you are like a crystal ball that has come into our lives for a reason, and we will do anything and everything that it takes to protect you."

A hot tear falls on my arm. Others build up on the rims of my eyes, waiting their turn to fall. Mrs. Chandler walks in and just looks at us.

"Is everything okay?"

"Everything's great," Mr. Chandler says, dropping the rubber balls into a box on the chair. "We were just talking about family."

"Can I call Anna?" I blurt.

Mrs. Chandler's lips just slightly curl up, raising my hopes. "Actually, I talked with Mrs. Craig today, Sara, and Anna had a little setback, so no, you can't call her yet. But she did have one bit of good news that she asked me to share with you, and that's that Anna put Abby back together by herself today."

"She did? That's great. That has to have earned her some points. Not many, maybe, but some, don't you think? It has to tell them that Anna might be getting better." They let me ramble without interrupting. "Were all the parts in the right places?" I look up at Mrs. Chandler.

"Not quite, but close. One step at a time, Sara. One step at a time," she answers.

That afternoon we go to see Dr. Kitanovski again. She really likes my drawing of Daddy.

"Who is this beside your papa?" she asks, pointing to a smaller shape.

"It's a shadow," I explain.

"And who is this shadow that stands all by itself by your papa?" she asks.

I look again and see that she's right. Daddy and his shadow don't touch.

When I look again, I see me.

I didn't know a person could hold so much crying inside, and when I let it all out, it is like water rushing from a broken faucet. Sometimes I can't breathe, I cry so hard, and Dr. Kitanovski rocks me, saying strange words. She never asks me to stop or be quiet. She just lets the river of tears flow.

When I finally stop, she reaches over and grabs

the white stone. "Did you think more about the white stone?" she asks.

"Kind of," I lie. "It's not rough like the others. It's smooth. Clean."

She sets the white stone down, and grabs the other two. "So, if this is how you see yourself, and this is how others see you, what might the white one be?"

I thought about Ben, and how no matter what I do, he never judges me. *Maybe the white stone is non-judging, but what's that in a person?*

"A non-judger?" I finally spout, rapidly running out of ideas.

She smiles a faraway smile, like something I said has triggered a thought. "A non-judger. I like that, Sara. Now picture this non-judger. What does that non-judger look like?"

"A tree," I blurt.

Her eyebrows shoot up. "A tree! Interesting. Why a tree?"

"I can be anything around a tree and it doesn't judge me. It just sits there and listens. It doesn't answer back, yell, make fun of me, cry, laugh . . . and it doesn't run away. It just sits and sways and stays," I add.

Her smile deepens. "Your non-judging tree I like." She hands me the white stone. "Keep this to remind you of it. And if you can't find a tree to sit under, talk to the stone and tell it your worries. See if you don't feel better."

"Are you sure?" I take the stone in my hand. It feels cool, and when I slip it into my pocket, it clinks against Ben's penny.

"I am sure."

September proves to be another month of getting used to things, including a new school where I feel lost without Anna, a new house, and the Chandler house rules: shoes off when entering, put one toy away before taking out another, wash your hands, no elbows on the table when eating, no talking with food in your mouth, say "please" and "thank you."

Every afternoon before supper, Kevin and I have to "take a walk on the wild side" and pick up after ourselves. And something else new is coming up: My first birthday without Anna is just around the corner.

"Sara," Mrs. Chandler says one morning while pouring herself a second cup of coffee. "Now that you are settled, we need to do something about your not being able to read very well."

I stop midgulp, letting a pool of orange juice just sit in my mouth. *She knows?* That means that the school will know soon, then the kids in my class. Faking it has become an art. I have everyone fooled. It's easy to become invisible in school. Sit in the back row and keep quiet. Get someone else to answer for me. Now what?

"Ben Silverman called. He's volunteering at the library, teaching kids and adults how to read. I was wondering if you wanted to go work with him."

"Ben? Really?" Suddenly everything looks better.

"Shall I take that as a yes?"

I nod, eager to see Ben again.

"The first class is at two o'clock this afternoon. Think you can get your chores done in time to go?"

It isn't going to take hours to clean my room. The closet will fit most of it. I nod.

By one thirty, she gathers her purse and keys. Hesitating at the door, she looks back, like she's forgotten something. "Nobody mentioned anything about bringing books. Of course, it's at the library, so I guess they have plenty to choose from. Still, if there's anything you want to take to read, better grab it now or forever hold your pizza."

I grin, not at her joke, but because there is something I want to take. I shake my head because I have it in my pocket, and I close the door behind us. If only Anna could come too. Then Ben could teach us both to read.

The library is full of muffled voices, shoes padding against the floor, and books being shuffled from shelves to tables. It has a smell like no other building. A dusty, leathery-book kind of smell. It's probably the cushy chairs I'm smelling. Whatever it is, I like it.

Mrs. Chandler and I wind our way through stacks of books to the back room. "I'll be waiting right here, or nearby. When you're done, just look around. You'll see me."

"Don't you want to come in and meet Ben?"

"We've already met—foster-parenting classes," she explains with a little wave of her hand. She then disappears behind a row of books.

I open the door and grin.

Ben stretches his arms wide. Never has a hug felt so good. I plaster my face against his shirt. He smells like laundry soap. A scruff of whiskers scratches my cheek when he kisses me. His whiskers smell like bacon. I breathe in a deep whiff of him and hold my breath, not wanting to let go.

"You don't mind that I called Mrs. Chandler and asked if she couldn't convince you to join the program?" His brown eyes sparkle.

"Me? Mind?" I can't stop grinning at him.

"Well, then! We'd better get started. Is there something special you want to read? A favorite book? A song, perhaps?"

Mama's letter pokes against my side. Ben studies my face. "Ah. I think there is something, yes? But you are afraid to show it to me?"

I nod and look out the window. People might see. We might get caught. The letter might end up lost or read by someone else. Mama might get caught and sent to jail.

Thoughts leapfrog all over the place.

Ben follows my gaze and looks back at me. "I have an idea," he whispers, pulling a book from the table. "Come over here by me and sit so that we are across from the window, looking out."

I pull a chair up beside him and sit down.

"Now, this something that you want to read. Put it here between the pages. If anyone from outside looks in, they'll think we're busy reading my magic book." He turns the cover toward me.

"The Magic Journey!"

Ben laughs. "You remember it?"

"How could I forget?" I unpin my pocket and carefully spread Mama's letter out on the table, then start to put it in Ben's book and stop.

"Your book is empty! What happened to the pictures? The stories?"

Ben smiles, closing the book around Mama's letter.

"You made up all these stories, didn't you, Ben? They were never in *The Magic Journey*."

"They were right here"—he taps his head—"and now they are here." He pats my head and opens the book to the page where I put the letter.

"Ah! This must be a letter from your mama, yes?"

I nod.

"And judging by all these wrinkles, you have had this letter a very long time?"

Again I nod.

Ben thinks for what feels like forever. Is he going to turn us in—me and Mama's letter? Finally, though, he puts his arm around my shoulder and clears his throat. "Okay. Let's start with the first line. Can you read any of the words?" He points a thick finger at the first word.

"'My dear Sara and Anna, this is a—'" I pause.

"Dif-fi-cult," Ben says, sounding out the word.

"'Difficult letter to write,'" I say carefully, then stop, since those are as many words as I know.

"Very good!" Ben gives me a little squeeze. "See there? You can read a little. This is good. This is very good."

"Can you read the rest of it to me?" I whisper.

Ben nods slowly. "I can, and I will. Then together we will read it, word by word, and you will know your mama's letter by heart. Along the way, we will learn things. Are you ready?"

My head nods yes, but my stomach knots up. It's not so sure.

Ben's deep voice pulls Mama's words from the page and plays them against the air like one of Daddy's sad songs. My heart beats fast, so fast I think it might break.

As he reads, I try to picture Mama writing the letter.

Is she sitting by a window, watching us from somewhere close by? Is she far away and remembering us in her thoughts? I search my own memory and see her long fingers wrapped around a strand of hair, blue veins standing out against her pale skin.

A memory tears at me. I try to push it away, but it comes back. Mama's biting her lower lip and squeezing me and Anna so tightly against her that I feel like my shoulders might crack. Our heads are touching, and she's whispering something.

I close my eyes and try to hear Ben, but another sound is smashing against my thoughts.

Bam, bam, bam.

I wince and try to push it away again.

Splinters of wood jump through the door like claws. I watch the wood crack under the pressure of an ax.

"I know you're in there, Rosie. Don't hurt my girls."

The voice is Daddy yelling at Mama, but he doesn't sound like himself. He's mad at her like he gets when he's been drinking.

Bam. Bam.

The sound is hollow through Mama's hand pressed against my ear.

"*You are angels,*" *she chants.* "*Angels flying up to heaven. Look how beautiful you are, dressed in white.*"

My face is pressed so tight against her chest that I can't breathe. The hard, cold toilet pushes against my back. We are squeezed between the toilet and the tub. The house offers no other hiding place.

"*God sees you and is smiling,*" *Mama whispers.* "*He's smiling because my girls are coming to see Him.*"

Crack. The wood splinters.

My lungs burn from not being able to breathe.

Let me go, Mama. Let me go.

"*See Him, Anna? Sara? God loves you.*" *She kisses the tops of our heads. I push hard, fighting for a breath, but I can't get away from her tight grip.*

At the last crash of wood, a door to my memory opens, spilling out secrets like a flood of light from a refrigerator. Was Mama trying to hurt us? And Daddy, was he trying to save us? I take a sudden breath and jerk.

Ben is holding me. He's not reading Mama's letter anymore. He's hugging me. "Breathe, Sara. Breathe. It's all right. Cry. Let it all come out. You'll feel better."

I look around. I'm not an angel. I'm at the library. I'm with Ben. I can breathe. I gasp for breath, coughing.

His deep voice helps me relax. When I'm calm, he smooths the paper out slowly, stroking it like he is stroking a cat. Then he picks it up in his big hands and quietly clears his throat. I sniff loudly, and he reminds me again to breathe in deep and to let the air out slowly. Then he starts the letter over again, and I hold on to Mama's every word:

My dear Sara and Anna,

This is a difficult letter to write. I am going to go away for a while. I know that running away isn't right, and I hope you will someday forgive me. I am leaving because everything I do is wrong, or so it feels like to me. I'm scared. Scared that I'm not a good mom. Scared that I can't protect you from all the things a parent is supposed to protect her children from. And so I run, hoping to give you a chance at a new and better life.

I sit here at my window, Sara, listening to a mockingbird sing one beautiful song after another, and for a moment, it's like having you here singing to me. I smile just thinking about you. Don't ever stop singing.

And Anna, I know you are hurting. I hope that someday you'll find the sweet person tucked away inside of you. You might think she's not there, but she is. One day you'll find her. I just know. Take care of one another.

I love you.

Mama

For a long time Ben and I don't say anything. Carefully, I fold up Mama's letter and put it back in my pocket. It turns out Rachel Silverman was right. It isn't my fault Mama left. She loves us. She thought she was somehow saving us. She was just scared and didn't know what to do.

"Sometimes," Ben says, his voice husky as he gives me a bear hug, "when we have not learned how to take good care of ourselves, we can't take good care of our children. This is how it was with your mama and papa. They love you and Anna with all their hearts. Of this I am sure. But they do not know how to take care of themselves, and because of this they do not know how to take care of you. You still miss them, yes?"

I nod, biting my tongue to keep from crying. "I let them down," I whisper.

Ben looks at me hard. "Let who down?"

"Mama. Daddy. I should never have gotten us caught. If I had found us a better hiding place, then Anna would be with me now, and Daddy could come home."

Ben shakes his head. "Maybe he would come home for a short time, but what about the next time he makes a mistake? And the next? How long were you to go on hiding like this? No, Sara. This is not your doing. You are a good daughter and a good sister and a good friend."

When he says "friend," I think about Lexie and how hard it is to be a friend. "I don't know how to be a friend," I whisper. "I've never had one or been one."

Ben smiles. "Ah, but you do know. You have been my friend for a long time now, yes? And it is time for you to meet kids your own age to become friends with. You will make someone a very, very good friend. I just hope they will be as good a friend to you."

I look at Ben, searching his face. "I did something else, too."

"What is this new something that is tearing you up inside?"

I swallow hard and take a deep breath, hold it, then slowly let it out. "I wished Anna would go away, and then she did. Now I might never see her again." I let the dreaded secret out.

Ben stares at his big fingers, then looks at me. "Breathe, Sara. I am going to tell you this, and you must believe me, yes?"

I nod.

"You could have said, 'Anna go, Anna stay,' and it would not have made one little bit of difference. None at all. It is your parents and the court that decide these things. Your parents made a poor choice. The courts took over. As for Anna, she hurts so much that she wants to hurt others—"

He pauses and pulls me back onto his lap. His chin comes to my shoulder. "She was hard to take care of all the time, yes?"

I look away. How did he know?

"Do not use energy to punish yourself for a feeling anyone would have. Use it instead to explore and learn new things."

"But what about Anna?"

A soft tap on the door announces that our time is

up. Outside the window, a boy waits his turn to learn to read. Ben gives me a small squeeze, and I go across the room to open the door.

"Same place on Wednesday?" Ben says, mostly to Mrs. Chandler, but also to me to remind me that I will be seeing him again in a few days.

"That sounds wonderful," she answers.

Ben bends down and whispers close to my ear. "Do you still have the penny?"

I nod, patting the pocket that holds Ben's penny, the white stone, and Mama's letter. He slips his big hand into a pocket and pulls out a small magnifying glass.

"Take this," he says, pressing it into my hand. "And tonight, take out the penny and read what it says on it. We'll talk about it on Wednesday, yes?"

I nod, wrapping my fingers around Ben's new gift.

On the drive home, I tell Mrs. Chandler about the letter and everything about Mama I can remember. She doesn't stop me or jump in to add things. She just listens, nodding and looking thoughtful every few sentences.

"Sounds like you and Ben had a great visit," she

finally says when no more words will come out of me.

I nod and then stare through the magnifying glass at my hand.

"What do you see?" Mrs. Chandler asks right as we pull into our driveway.

"Lines. Lots of lines. Just like in a dream catcher," I answer.

And she smiles.

That night, I sound out some of the words on the penny. "In . . . God . . . we . . . trust."

In God we trust!

I did it. I read the words all by myself!

CHAPTER 26

LIVING SO CLOSE TO LEXIE IS ALMOST LIKE HAVING a sister. It also means that Sneaker lives close by, and I can see her every day.

Even though Lexie isn't my sister, she can talk about things in a way that Anna can't. In full sentences, even. Ben said that I'd make a great friend to someone, but sometimes being friends with Lexie feels like I'm being unfair to Anna. It doesn't seem fair that she can't be with us and have Lexie as her friend too.

She's not you, Anna. Nobody could ever be you. It's something I say every time I head for Lexie's house. Somehow, just saying it makes me feel better.

"What will happen when all the kids find out I can't read?" I ask Lexie on the way to school.

"You can read, Sara, just not fast. That's why you're in that special reading class. There's nothing bad about being in there."

"Easy for you to say. You can read."

"I'll read with you every day after school, if you want," Lexie says. "I'll help if you want me to."

"*Kevin* can read better than I can. If I could read, I'd be able to write better too."

Lexie stares at me and I have to look away. "I miss Anna."

Lexie squeezes my shoulder. "Me too, and I don't even know her. If you learn to read and write, you can write Anna letters and tell her about all the stuff that we do. It will be like having her here, in a way."

I shake my head. "Nothing will be like having her here except really having her here. Everything else is pretending, and I'm tired of pretending."

Lexie nods and gives my shoulder another squeeze.

Friday, a week later, Lexie and I are walking home from school. We stuck together like glue all week.

As we near our homes, a car swerves and honks its horn at a stray racing across the road.

"There are too many homeless cats!" I say to Lexie. "Can't we do something?"

"Like what?" Lexie looks up suddenly, and Skeeter whizzes past us on his Rollerblades, waving a net in the air, trying to catch something for his growing bug collection. In his other hand he holds a plastic jar.

Lexie watches him for a minute, her eyes narrowing. When Skeeter opens the jar and puts a bug in, she comes unglued.

"Why do you have to kill them?" she shouts.

Skeeter gives her a pained look. "It's a bit hard to pin a moving bug to a chart," he answers, skidding to a stop.

"Why do you have to pin them and label them in the first place? Can't you just learn what they are and let them live? What if someone came and caught *you* in a net and pinned you to a stupid piece of cardboard and wrote 'Skeeter' underneath? How would you feel?"

Skeeter rolls his eyes. "I guess I'd feel fine, as long as they wrote 'Chip Culicidae Anderson' under me." Culicidae, he explains to me, is the scientific name for mosquito. "Got any better ideas for collecting bugs?" he snaps, glaring at Lexie.

"As a matter of fact, I do. Don't put alcohol in the jar. After you catch them, I'll draw them. You can label the drawing, then let them go."

Skeeter makes a face. "I'll think about it." But I notice he makes no move to set the bug he's already caught free.

"Course, Dad might not be so happy with you," he calls over his shoulder before heading up their driveway.

"What's Dad got to do with this?"

"You want me to set free the very bug that's killing our pine trees?" He seems pleased that he's figured out something that we don't know anything about. "A spittlebug, to be exact," he adds, examining the newest prisoner.

I look at him, amazed.

"The Internet and bug books," Lexie says, reading my mind. "Hundreds and hundreds of bug books. He lives for bugs—and the longer he lives, the more bugs die."

She looks at Skeeter. "Pine tree or no pine tree, I still don't think you should kill them."

"Whatever." He disappears into the house, jar and all.

"Brothers!" she grumbles. "Okay, now, what were you saying about the strays?"

"That we should do something . . . maybe we could start a club. You know, like a . . ." I think for a minute. "What about a foster care club for cats?"

Lexie's face breaks into a huge smile. "Sara! That's great! We could make flyers and posters, and we could dress up like cats for Halloween and go door-to-door collecting money for the Humane Society or something!"

Lexie is talking so fast that I almost can't understand her, but then she stops. "We're going to need a name for our club."

"How about Paws?" I ask, looking at her to see her reaction.

She grins. "Paws! Purr-fect!"

We laugh. "A Cause for Paws," she adds, buzzing around me like she's a big mosquito herself.

"Okay, now we have a name, but how will this work? If we catch the strays, then what?" We reach the steps to her porch, and I watch a calico kitten slip under a hole in a board.

Inside, Lexie heads straight for the kitchen, where

her mom is pulling out a sheet of fresh-baked cookies. I breathe in the smell, hold it, and let it out slowly.

"Help yourself," Mrs. Anderson says, smiling. Unlike Lexie, her hair is blond and her eyes a catlike green. Her smile is quick and warm. "Are you by any chance talking about the stray kittens?"

Lexie and I both nod.

"The real problem is that people let their cats have all those kittens in the first place, don't you think?" She lifts the fresh-baked cookies off the cooled sheet with a spatula and pushes a plate of warm cookies toward us. We each grab two at a time. The chocolate chips melt over my tongue.

"Yeah," Lexie mumbles, breaking a Chandler rule by talking with food in her mouth.

I swallow a bite of cookie. "We thought maybe we could start a sort of foster program for animals. You know—help find homes for them."

Lexie's mom's eyebrows rise. "That's a nice idea."

Skeeter appears out of nowhere and creeps up on a cricket that has come into the kitchen. His hands close gently around it.

"Don't kill it," Lexie reminds him.

Skeeter grins and puts the cricket in a jar. "I won't. See? No alcohol. Just leaves for it to munch on."

Lexie relaxes in the chair. "Brothers are trainable. Who knew?" she whispers when he leaves.

For two days, Lexie and I take up the kitchen table at her house, figuring out how a foster program for stray kittens might work. Posters we've made to hang in store windows and at 7-Eleven flank the walls. Bits of colored paper, glue, glitter, staples, tape, and ribbon decorate the table and floor as we try to put together a flyer explaining our mission.

"You could write, 'Who, what, where, when, and why,'" I suggest. We'd just learned about this in my reading class.

"Yeah. The 'who' could be who gets the strays," she answers, pencil poised. Skeeter walks in.

"How about old people?" he says, answering Lexie's question. We both laugh. Skeeter frowns but keeps talking.

"Remember how Gramma used to hug that old teddy bear like it was real?" He stuffs a gummy worm in his mouth and holds the bag out to me. I take one.

"She thought it was real." Lexie reaches for a worm.

"Maybe kids in special places like Anna's could have kittens too." I bite into the candy.

"Who decides those kinds of things?" Skeeter asks. Lexie and I shrug.

"I'll ask Dad." Lexie starts making a list. "He's an investigative reporter. He knows stuff like that."

"Your dad's a spy?" Goose bumps chase up my arm. I stop gluing cat prints to the flyer and stare at her.

"Yeah, I guess you could say that." Lexie holds up a Wanted poster she made that has a photo of a kitten on it.

Skeeter holds up a finished flyer. "You should put these around the neighborhood, reminding people to get their cats fixed."

"That's the plan." Lexie takes it from him. "Or to remind them to keep closer track of their cats so no unwanted kittens are born," she adds.

"Who says they're unwanted?" I bristle. "Maybe lots of people want them, but they just don't have a way to get them. We can have them, you know, come to the house so we can see if they'll be good to the kittens. If they pass our test, they can get one. If not, then they don't." I look to see their reaction. After all, I know the foster system well.

Lexie finishes her list and draws a new line down the page. "That plan might work for all the stray kittens in our own neighborhood, but we'd have to catch them, cage them, and feed them. That could cost big bucks. I think we should try to get most of them into places like old people's homes." She writes *To Do* at the top of the new column.

I'm secretly proud that I can read what she has written—upside down, even.

"And therapeutic foster homes," I remind her, remembering the words Mrs. Chandler used to explain where Anna might have to go after leaving the residential center. The key word was "might."

"Foster cats for foster homes. Hey, I like it!" Lexie punches me in the arm.

Later that afternoon, after we've gathered all our supplies, piled up the posters, and stacked the flyers, Skeeter lets me borrow his bike so that Lexie and I can ride over to the Humane Society office to see if they already have programs like ours. We're out of breath when we get there. They don't have a similar program. We leave a stack of the flyers we made for them to distribute, which they seem happy to do. In exchange, they give us a tour of the shelter.

"Oh, isn't he cute? Don't you just want to scoop them all up and take them home?" Lexie sticks her finger in a cage and lets a puppy lick it. She looks at me. "Hey, did I say something wrong?"

"What's wrong is that I haven't thought about Anna in days."

"So, let me get this straight. You're supposed to live only half a life because the other half isn't there?"

I stare at her. "I don't know, okay? I don't know what to do or what to think or what to be. All I know is that I have a family, a friend, a home, a pet, even. But my sister is locked up somewhere with nothing and nobody."

"You don't know that," Lexie snaps. "She might have friends. She might feel at home where she is."

I put up my hand to stop her. Dogs yip, bark, and claw at their cages trying to get our attention. "You're right. I don't know, Lex, but neither do you."

"You know what? Your mind's somewhere else. Let's just go." Lexie races past the dogs, through the cat section, and out of the animal shelter with me close behind.

"Fine." I stomp after her, not knowing why I feel so mad. But I do. Lexie's mad too, probably at me, but who cares?

We barely talk on the bike ride home. I give Skeeter his bike back, and he looks from one of us to the other. Something seems to tell him not to ask questions.

I turn to leave.

"Do you want to meet after school tomorrow? We can make more flyers." Lexie looks and sounds like nothing's happened.

"Sure. I guess." I back away. "Unless you want to come over and make some now."

"I'll ask."

I wait. Less than a minute later, Lexie and I are walking home.

As we walk in the front door, the phone rings, and I motion for her to wait. "Hang on, Lex." *Please be Anna. Please be Anna.* I pick up the phone.

"Hello?" I say. I'm suddenly so nervous, my hands start to sweat. What if she doesn't recognize my voice and hangs up?

"Hello?" The voice answering isn't Anna's. "May I speak to Sara, please?"

"This is Sara." I sigh and motion for Lexie to come listen, mouthing that it isn't Anna after all. We press our heads together trying to hear.

SARA LOST AND FOUND

The woman's voice says, "Hi, Sara. This is Heather White from KUNV radio. We're doing a special show on strays in our community. Elmer Wiley from the Humane Society gave me your name. He said you have a club that's involved with bringing attention to animals in need?"

I grin at Lexie. "Yes. It's called A Cause for Paws, and right now we're trying to do something about the stray kittens in our neighborhood."

"That's wonderful. Do you think you could come to the radio station for an interview? We'd really like to hear what your plans are."

I look at Lexie, my eyes wide. "Just a sec," I say, and I press the phone to my chest so I can talk to her. "Do you want to go?"

Lexie nods.

"Can my friend Lexie Anderson come? She's the president of the club and has lots of great ideas."

"President?" Lexie whispers. I grin and wave for her to be quiet, then turn my attention back to the phone.

"Sure. What time do you girls get out of school?"

"Three o'clock."

"Would tomorrow afternoon at four be a good time?"

I cup my hand over the receiver. "Tomorrow after school at four?"

Lexie shrugs and nods.

"Do you know how to get here?" Heather asks.

I cup my hand over the phone again. "Get a piece of paper and a pencil. Out of that drawer. No, not that one, the one beside it."

"What for?"

"Directions."

"Dad knows how to get there."

"Are you sure?"

"I'm sure, Sara."

"That's okay. We know how to get there," I practically shout. After I say good-bye and hang up, Lexie and I jump up and down, screaming.

"We're famous!" she shouts.

"I'll be right back. I want to go tell Edi—I mean Mrs.—"

Lexie's look is sympathetic. "It must be weird not knowing what to call your parents."

I nod. "Very weird," I say as I leave the room.

When I come back, I'm all out of breath from running. "They want to go with us, but Mrs. Chandler has to take Kevin to the dentist, and Mr. Chandler said he has to be in court. They said to see if your dad can take us and to remember to say all that please-and-thank-you stuff before, during, and after the interview."

"Yeah, yeah." Lexie grins. "We will!"

That night, when my head hits the pillow, I know sleep is going to be impossible. I've never been on the radio before. Maybe Anna will hear me! And what about Daddy?

I picture Daddy's face when he turns on the radio and hears me talking.

Will he call the station? Or maybe come and get me?

Tomorrow can't come fast enough.

CHAPTER 27

LEXIE AND I CAN'T STOP TALKING ON THE RIDE TO the radio station. "I think we should mention about getting the old people's home to adopt kittens. What do you think?" She looks across the seat at me.

"Do we have to go through Congress or something to get it okayed or to get a law passed?"

Lexie gets a thinking look on her face. She knows I have a point. Everyone has rules. The question is, who rules old people?

"I don't know," she admits. "Let's ask Dad." She leans over and taps his shoulder. Mr. Anderson turns down the radio and looks at her in the rearview mirror.

"You tapped?"

"Dad. Are old people's homes owned by the old people?"

"They can be, but they generally aren't. They're usually privately owned businesses. Why?"

"Because we want to plan something that involves people in old people's homes, and we were wondering if we needed to have Congress pass a law or something."

Her dad smiles. "No. But you would have to get permission from the individual facilities."

"How many old people's homes are there in Oakview?"

"First of all, ladies, the more politically correct name for old people is either 'seniors' or 'elderly,'" he explains. "And the places they live are more commonly called 'senior residence centers' or 'convalescent homes.' As for how many of them there are in Oakview, I don't really know. Probably a dozen. Maybe even two." He rounds a curve, and I lean hard toward Lexie. The seat belt tightens against me.

Both of us groan. "This is going to be a lot more work than we thought."

I shift my weight, trying to get comfortable, just as Mr. Anderson turns into the radio station's parking lot.

I look across the car at Lexie. "If it means someone

has a kitten and a kitten has a home, I think it's worth it. Don't you?"

"Depends."

She never says what it depends on, and my thoughts turn to the interview. How can something that makes so much sense—helping kittens and lonely people—turn into something so hard to do?

Heather White helps us relax by giving us cookies and milk. Then she shows us some of the questions she's going to ask. I just nod a lot, not wanting anyone to realize I can't read fast enough to know the questions she's showing us. Before long, it's time to go on the air.

"Good luck, girls," Mr. Anderson whispers, hugging Lexie and giving me a big smile. "Just be yourselves. You'll do great."

Lexie grabs my hands in hers and squeezes tight. "A Cause for Paws," she whispers.

"A Cause for Paws," I whisper back.

Heather leads us into the studio, puts our headsets on, and tests our voices. As each of us speaks, she raises and lowers levers on what she calls an equalizer until she is satisfied that everything sounds just right.

Like magic, music comes on, making it sound like something really special is about to happen. As the music starts to fade, Heather smiles brightly at us and winks.

"Thank you for joining us today on 'A Closer Look.' I'm your host, Heather White, and with me today are two delightful guests with a heartfelt cause. I hope you'll listen to what they have to say and offer them support. I'm leaving the phone lines open, so feel free to call with questions, comments, or suggestions. The number to call is 555-KUNV.

"Our special guests today are Sara Olson and Lexie Anderson, organizers and cofounders of A Cause for Paws—a humanitarian club made up of kids working hard to improve the quality of life for the strays in our neighborhoods. Welcome, ladies."

"Thank you," we say together, and stifle our giggles. Lexie looks as nervous as I feel.

"Now, then. Your club sounds great, but what exactly do you do?" Heather focuses first on me.

"Well, we started A Cause for Paws because we wanted to do something about all the stray cats in our neighborhood. When people don't have their cats fixed,"

I add, relaxing a little, "the cats have kittens. Then the kittens grow up and have kittens, and those kittens grow up to have more kittens. . . ."

"Whose job do you think it is to care for and feed all those unwanted animals?" Heather asks Lexie.

Lexie leans closer to the microphone and shoots an uneasy glance toward me. She knows I bristle at the word "unwanted."

"I think it's the job of the people who didn't take care of their cats."

"In other words, you would place the responsibility on the cat owners?"

Lexie nods. Heather covers her microphone and whispers, "Remember to talk, not nod. People can't see you."

"Yes," Lexie blurts. "The problem is the cat owners."

"So, your club is trying to fix the existing problem of all these unwanted kittens running around, and prevent the problem from happening again. That's a pretty tall order."

"These kittens aren't unwanted," I say, trying to keep my voice steady. "Maybe people who want them just don't know how to get them."

Lexie beams at me. It turns out to be the perfect lead-in for announcing our plan.

"What do you think can be done?" Heather asks.

Both of us talk at once. "We have this idea," Lexie says.

"It's in the early stages," I add. "But if we could get someone to help us, someone who knows about rules and laws and stuff—"

Lexie clears her throat. "Yeah, if we could get people to think about how scared and hungry these kittens must be out there all on their own, and how we have a lot of lonely people in the city who would love to have a pet, then we could try to put two and two together."

"We call it our Foster Kitten, Foster Home Program," I ad-lib. "We're hoping that if people keep the kittens for a while and grow to like them, they'll want to adopt them." One of the phone lines lights up, and Lexie and I stare at it, mesmerized. Someone out there is listening!

Heather presses a button to take the call. "'A Closer Look.' Hi, you're on the air."

"Hello, Heather. My name is Audrey Davis. I'm a local veterinarian, and I listen to your program regularly.

I work closely with the Humane Society and other animal rescue groups, and I just had to call and say how impressed I am with your guests. As a matter of fact, I'd like to offer my clinic this Saturday from one p.m. to four p.m. so that A Cause for Paws can bring kittens by for a checkup, shots, and spaying and neutering. I challenge fellow veterinarians to make the same pledge to help these kids out. Let's support worthy programs like this."

Lexie and I can barely believe our ears. More calls come in. One listener volunteers to contact the Humane Society and other animal-protection agencies to ask them to sponsor more Cause for Paws clubs in neighborhoods throughout the city. Another call comes in from the general manager of High Sierra Convalescent Center, who agrees to adopt two kittens as soon as Dr. Davis examines them. He asks other convalescent homes to do it too.

Finally, Heather turns to us. "Before we conclude today's program, are there any last thoughts you'd like to share?"

I stare at the button that lights up when a call comes in. Why hasn't Daddy called? How can I get his attention now that the show's almost over?

"I've got something," I blurt. Heat races to my face. "I know a song and, well, maybe if I sing it, everyone will remember what we talked about today. I'd like to sing it for all the strays out there who are lost, lonely, and wanting or needing a home."

Lexie's mouth drops open. "You can sing?" she whispers.

Heather smiles and announces to the listeners, "Well, this is a treat. A closing song written and sung by Sara Olson."

"Actually, it's like one my daddy wrote," I correct, hoping beyond all hope that by stretching things out, he will hear me and figure out how to find me.

"You're on, Sara."

I clear my throat. My hands start to sweat. What should I sing? I would have to make up a song on the spot. Maybe Anna will hear it along with Daddy.

"My song's called 'Home,'" I say. I open my mouth and out come the words:

Home is a place
I wish I could be.
Right now my home

257

Isn't up to me.
You ran away.
My heart broke in two.
Now I have no home,
And I don't have you.
Home is a place
I wish I could be.
Right now my home
Is inside of me.
My home's my heart,
And it's on the mend.
Invite me home,
And you've made a friend.

"Adopt a stray!" I say, ending my song.

"Wow, Sara," Lexie whispers, all choked up. "It's like a theme song!"

After a moment of silence, more phone lines light up and the closing music comes on. "A Closer Look" is over.

After we thank Heather, Lexie and I take off the headsets. Exhausted, we head back to the front of the studio, where Lexie's dad is waiting for us, smiling. I look around, hoping to see my dad, too, but he's nowhere. I have to think of a way to give him enough time to find the station.

"You did it!" Lexie shouts, hugging me.

"We did it," I correct, hugging her back. Suddenly I realize what having a friend feels like. The feeling is wonderful, yet scary. Friends can disappear too. Like sisters, and brothers, and pets, and parents. They can be there one minute and gone the next.

"You sure did." Heather beams. She walks us to the door and shakes our hands. "I might just have to come over and take one of those kittens myself," she says, giving me a hug.

"Ready?" Lexie's dad asks, his eyes sparkling.

"I have to go to the bathroom," I say quickly.

"It's right down the hall, Sara." Heather points down a shiny hallway. "And to your left," she adds. I walk slowly. Behind me, Lexie is chattering with her dad. I don't even have to turn around to picture them grinning at each other.

When I come out, Daddy will be here. I just know it.

"Did you, like, die and flush yourself down the toilet?" a voice suddenly calls. I stay seated, chin on my elbows, and don't answer. I know it's Lexie.

"Sara?" Lexie's hair sweeps the floor as she bends down to look under the stall door. "I thought those were your feet. You okay?"

I sigh. It seems answer enough. I open the door and look for some sign on her face that Daddy came. It's like she reads my mind.

"He's not here, Sara."

I start for the door. "Hey, don't you want to wash your hands?"

"I didn't go," I mumble. "I was just—"

I don't have to finish. Part of being a friend, it turns out, is knowing what someone can't say and why they can't say it. Lexie knows. Right now, that's enough.

On the drive home, I listen to Lexie talk everything over with her dad. I watch their faces light up and the sparkle in their eyes dance.

Daddy should have been there. He didn't come. My thoughts shift, not to Mama or seeing Daddy, but to Anna. All I want to do is see my sister. At least I know where she is.

The car suddenly gets quiet. I look up.

"Are you all right?" Lexie looks at me funny.

I don't realize until then that I've been crying. "I was so sure Daddy would hear me and that he'd be at the station."

Lexie looks at her dad and back at me. I can tell she's struggling for something to say. "The biggest thing I ever lost is a tooth," she says, "but another one grew in its place. It's not like losing a person."

"With all those rules about Anna having to improve her behavior, I'll probably never get to see her or even talk to her again." I bite my lip.

Mr. Anderson pulls over to the side of the road and twists around to look at me. "I have something that might make you feel better," he says, reaching into his pocket. He hands me my half-heart necklace.

At first I just stare. "It can't be!" I say, but it is. I run my finger over the half heart, knowing Anna's running her finger over her half.

"How did you find it?"

"We were sweeping out the attic where the box was that you hid Anna's sheets in—the one with Cowwy?" Lexie says excitedly.

I nod, clinging to the necklace.

"Well, when Dad went to toss the dirt we swept up, guess what he saw?"

"My necklace! You found my necklace. Thank you. Thank you so much."

Lexie grins. "We found it, *and* I had Mom get a new chain for it. The one it had was broken, but it's not anymore! See?"

I put it on. "This is so great. My mom gave this to me and the other half to Anna. She said to never take it off, but my chain broke. Anna still has hers." Words slide out of me like water over rocks. Mr. Anderson smiles and pulls back onto the road.

"Now you don't have to take it off either. And Dad can help you get in to see Anna, right, Dad?"

I hold my breath, not daring to breathe, waiting for his answer.

"*Who-o-a!* Slow down, Lex. I didn't say that—"

"But you said—"

He holds a hand up like a stop sign. "Let's tackle one problem at a time, shall we?"

As we pull into the Andersons' driveway, a photographer from the local paper is waiting for us. I see the Chandlers waving from Lexie's porch. We jump out of the car and gather in the front yard. Kevin starts handing out stray kittens.

"One for you. . . . One for you."

The photographer has me, Kevin, Skeeter, and Lexie hold the kittens out like we're wanting to give them to someone. "Look for it in tomorrow's paper," he says, packing up his gear.

Tomorrow's paper! *Maybe Daddy will see my picture and then come get me!* The thought gets my heart pounding so hard, I can feel it.

"Thank you!" Lexie and I shout together.

On our way home, Kevin tells me about all the Halloween decorations he's made for the house. When he takes a breather, Mrs. Chandler gives my shoulders a squeeze. "You were great on the radio, Sara. I am so proud of you."

"You heard me?"

She nods. I hold up the necklace for her to see. "Mr. Anderson found it in the attic at their house."

"Let me see, let me see." Kevin jumps in front of me for a closer look. I bend over and show him.

He turns and pulls his dad's arm down for a whisper. "Should I tell her the heart's broke?"

Mr. Chandler scruffs Kevin's hair. "She knows," he whispers back. "The necklace was made that way."

"Oh," Kevin answers, but I know he doesn't understand.

I walk beside them, happy about my necklace and how great it feels to get back something I thought I had lost, and how happy I am to be part of a family that really loves me and cares about what I'm doing and feeling.

Later, back at home, as I put Mama's photo and letter, Ben's penny, and Abby's plastic arm in the box that Pablo gave me, I feel something else, too.

A sense of hope.

CHAPTER 28

THE NEXT MORNING, LEXIE RACES OVER, WAVING the paper wildly. "Look, Sara! There really is a story about us in the *Oakview Daily News*!" She hands it to me, and I can't believe my eyes. Along with the photo is a story all about A Cause for Paws.

"We'll get copies and frame them!" Lexie announces, eyeing Mr. Chandler's thin French pancakes. He invites her to join us, and we wolf them down. Between bites, we talk about new ways to make our foster kitten program a success. But the whole time we're eating and talking, I'm smiling inside. Daddy will see my picture. Daddy will take me home.

At school, kids crowd around us, taking flyers faster

than we can pass them out. One kid even asks me to sign the flyer. I sign it *Sara Olson*. My writing's not very good, but he doesn't seem to care.

On Saturday, Dr. Davis gives the kittens checkups, and she even keeps a lot of them at the animal hospital so people can go there to adopt them.

A local pet store called Meow 'N' Friends supplies a month's worth of free cat food to High Sierra Convalescent Center, and KUNV continues to mention our Cause for Paws campaign on their public service announcements.

To prepare for Halloween on Monday, Mr. Chandler steps up onto a ladder to hang a hairy spider over the front door to scare the trick-or-treaters. Mrs. Chandler adjusts the tail on Kevin's dragon costume. Kevin wiggles and shakes.

"Be still, Kev, if you want this tail to last the night."

Kevin grins and finally settles down.

"Sara? We have something important to talk to you about," Mrs. Chandler says.

I look up from a nose-and-whiskers mask I'm making for my cat costume and see them lined up like birds on a wire, looking down at me. My chest tightens.

"Like what?" I figure I know what's coming. They're moving, or another kid needs a placement and they can't keep me, or . . . they don't want to be a foster family anymore. But their faces don't look like bad news.

"Like whether you'd like to become a more permanent part of our family."

"You mean—" I don't finish the thought.

Mrs. Chandler steps toward me and smiles. "We'd like to adopt you, Sara. It's not going to happen overnight. We'll need letters of release from your mother and father, and the paperwork is a nightmare, but if it's all right with you, we really want you to join our family."

We'd like to adopt you. The magic words dance in my head. "Adopt me?" My mind whirls. They want me!

"What about Anna?" I watch an uneasy look pass between Mr. and Mrs. Chandler.

Mr. Chandler walks over and sits down beside me on the couch. Kevin is as quiet as he's ever been and stares at his dad.

"We don't want you to think we're not being honest with you, Sara, so I'll tell you that it would be very hard for us to take Anna right now. She needs—" Mr. Chandler looks at his wife for the right phrase.

"Special help?" I fill in the blank for him while everything in me collapses. "Can I just see her?" I watch the spider's shadow dance on the wall behind them, as if it, too, is trying to get away from something. The truth, maybe.

"We won't say you can," Mr. Chandler explains gently, "but we won't say you can't, either, because the fact is, right now we simply don't know."

"We're working with Mrs. Craig and the residential center to see if there's a possibility of working out visitations," Mrs. Chandler adds, "but I won't lie to you, Sara. These things take time."

I nod. I know how long everything takes. They don't need to tell me.

A thought troubles me, though. *If they adopt me, do I keep my last name? Or will I have to change it to theirs?*

"If you adopt me, what will I be called?"

"We don't need to decide that now. But even if you keep your last name, when we adopt you, you'll be a member of our family," Mr. Chandler adds, urging Kevin to come sit with him. Kevin lifts his dragon feet high and tromps across the room. He plops down hard on his dad's lap.

When we adopt you. There they are again. The magic words. I think back to Pablo and how he must have felt. Still, their questions leave me feeling funny inside. If I give up my last name, am I giving up on my family? On Anna? *You're an Olson, Sara. You'll always be an Olson. Never forget that.*

Daddy's words ring in my ears.

I try to think of times other people change their names. Criminals sometimes change their names. I've stolen things, so that kind of fits, but I don't want to feel like a criminal. Actors and musicians sometimes use other names. I want to be a singer, so that kind of fits.

Women change their names when they get married. Well, it'll be a long time before I get married, but then I remember something else. Sometimes women hyphenate their old names with their new ones. Maybe I could be Sara Olson-Chandler. That way, if they ever came back to get me, Mama and Daddy would see I not only kept my name, but I also kept my word.

Mrs. MacMillan would have liked the sound of that—keeping my word.

"You still look worried, Sara. Is it about your name? You don't need to decide anything about that now." Mrs. Chandler stands and offers me a hand to stand too. I grab it and pull myself to my feet. Her eyes are warm and loving, but I see hurt in them. I know she had hoped my answer would be "Yes, I want to be part of this family!" without any hesitation.

I walk over and hug her, not wanting to see the pain anymore. I feel Kevin's arms wrap around us from behind.

I lie awake that night, thinking about the bed on the floor at my old house and the cold rooms. The empty cupboards.

Since moving in with the Chandlers, I've found Sneaker, made friends with Lexie and Skeeter, learned to read with Ben Silverman, started a new school—and now, I might even get adopted.

In a way, it's like magic. One minute you don't belong anywhere, and the next you're a member of a family. I remind myself of what Mrs. Chandler said about it taking a long time, and how Mama and Daddy would have to give up their rights to me. Just thinking the words—*give up their rights*—makes me want to cry.

Instead, I slip out of bed and stand by the mirror. "Sara Olson-Chandler," I whisper. "Sara Olson-Chandler. What do you think, Cowwy? Should I make a brand-new start with a brand-new name?" I press her against my cheek and search her one-eyed, pouty face for an answer.

"Meow," I answer for her.

I crawl back into bed. It's so warm and soft—the way beds are supposed to feel—and for some strange reason, I'm reminded of that first bite into a slice of hot buttered toast. The blanket wraps around me like one of Daddy's old hugs. As I drift off to sleep, I run my fingers across the half-heart necklace around my neck and pull Cowwy close.

"I bet they even know that tomorrow isn't just Halloween. It's my eleventh birthday," I whisper.

CHAPTER 29

AS I HEAD DOWNSTAIRS THE NEXT MORNING, I hear voices in the kitchen.

"Shhhhh! She'll hear us."

"Ow, Kevin! You stepped on my foot."

"Sorry."

"Skeeter, move over. I can't straighten out my leg."

"Want me to pull it? Pull your leg, get it?"

"I don't get it," Kevin whispers.

"Shhhh! Here she comes."

Silence.

"Surprise!"

If my mouth opens any wider, it could fit a grape-fruit in it. The kitchen is full of stray cats, a dragon, a couple of witches, a vampire, and a goblin. Of course, I recognize the voices of Lexie, Skeeter, Kevin, and all the grown-ups. I scan the masks, hoping to see Anna hiding under one of them. It would be the best surprise of all. But she's not there.

"Happy birthday!" everyone shouts at once.

"Thanks." I force a smile. "I don't know what to say."

"Say cheese!" Mr. Anderson calls out, clicking the camera. The flash almost blinds me.

"Cheese," I say too late.

"Make a wish," Mrs. Chandler says, bringing out a cake shaped just like a black Halloween cat, with *Happy Birthday, Sara* written in orange, my favorite color. I can't help thinking about my last cake—a mound of mashed potatoes with a candle in the middle. I love mashed potatoes. It was a great cake. Especially since Anna had made it for me all by herself exactly one year ago.

"Wish for something good," Skeeter says as Mrs. Chandler lights the candles. "But don't tell anyone, or it won't come true."

"Wait!" My foster dad reaches across the table, then lights and adds one more candle to the cake. "Here's one for good luck."

I take a deep breath and blow with all my heart. My wish is a very big wish. Everyone starts singing "Happy Birthday." Presents appear from nowhere.

"Let's open some gifts now, but save others for later," Mr. Chandler suggests. "There's somewhere we need to go."

My heart races.

"Yeah, there's this Halloween carnival downtown," Kevin says, clapping his hands. "And it has a giant Ferris wheel. You go so high up, you can see the whole city. Your stomach will flip-flop. You might even throw up! I did last year."

I try not to show my disappointment. A carnival? That wasn't my wish.

But then I think about Ben's story about the nine-story cat and how different things can look from different angles. Maybe going on the biggest Ferris wheel would help me see things better.

"Hey, you're not giving the whole day away, are you?" Mr. Chandler picks up a package and hands it to Kevin. "I thought your job was to give Sara her presents!"

"Oh, yeah." Kevin passes the package to me. It's an iPod with earbuds for listening to music. A song is already in it. I press the button, and on comes my song, "Home."

Drums and piano have been added on top of my singing. It's magical.

"Heather recorded it for you," Mr. Chandler says when the song has finished. "She said to wish you the happiest of birthdays."

"And we did!" Kevin shouts. "Now can we have some cake?"

"You can have cake later, when Sara opens her other presents," Mr. Chandler says.

Kevin groans, but the Andersons take his cue and head for home.

"My present's coming later," Lexie whispers as she files past. She squeezes my arm.

"Mine too." Skeeter laughs.

"Like you really have one," Lexie quips, bumping against her brother.

"Who says I don't?"

I smile after the door closes and turn to see my new family all smiling back at me. "Wow. Thanks— Mom, Dad, Kev. This is great. The party, the presents, the cake."

Mrs. Chandler's face melts into a hesitant smile. "Does this mean—"

"I think so," I answer, feeling suddenly awkward. But for the first time in a long time, the words "Mom" and "Dad" feel okay to say.

"I got a real sister! I got a real sister!" Kevin sings, dancing around the table.

"If it's okay with you, I want my name to be Sara Olson-Chandler."

"Okay with us?" From the looks on their faces and their hugs, tears, and laughter, I feel like I've given *them* a birthday present.

"I'll get right on it," Dad says, starting for the phone.

"And I'll get right on the cake!" Kevin shouts, making everyone laugh.

By the end of the day, I'm so tired, I can hardly move my legs. I plug the best present I got—new earbuds— into my ears and listen to more songs.

Lexie comes in second with the picture of us in the newspaper in a frame. She also gives me a tattered book called *Dicey's Song*. I look at the print and hesitate.

"It looks harder than it is," she says. "You'll see. It's a great book."

Skeeter gives me his prize catch: a beautiful orange-and-black monarch butterfly that he's framed and labeled. "I didn't even have to kill it. It was already dead when I found it," he tells me, grinning. The card with it says, *All the better to bug you with.* I grin back.

Still, my biggest wish is the one thing I didn't get.

Lexie stops by to see if I want to go trick-or-treating door-to-door to collect for the SPCA. But I feel so sure that Anna is going to show up, I tell her I'd rather stay home.

Every time the doorbell rings and a chorus of "Trick or treat!" filters through the windows, I race to open the door, studying every one of the trick-or-treaters, even the ones who are too short or too tall, hoping that one of the hidden faces might be Anna's. After an hour of searching, I give up.

Kevin and Dad return from trick-or-treating with a whole pillowcase full of candy.

"I'll share with you, Sara," the droopy dragon promises.

"Share cavities," Dad grumbles. "Shall we take one last drive and end the big day with some ice cream?"

"Ice cream!" Kevin jumps up and down.

I force a smile, twisting a strand of hair around my finger. Ice cream is not what I wished for either.

A full moon lights up the October sky. I spot a star—the one right by the moon—and wish my big wish for the thousandth time that day.

As we pass Lexie's house, I see her through the window, still dressed like a cat and chasing Skeeter around the front room.

"We think we should tell you something, Sara," my new mom says, breaking through Kevin's excited chatter about all the goblins and creatures he saw. "I know Lexie and her family wanted it to be a big surprise and all, but I don't want you to be unprepared."

"Unprepared for what?" I ask, sensing that something bad is going to happen. Have they changed their minds already about the adoption?

"Unprepared to see Anna," she says quietly.

"Anna? See her?" I force myself to breathe.

"Mrs. Craig says that Anna's supervisor needs to test Anna's behavior around family—around you."

At first, no words come out. Then: "I can't wait for you to meet her," I blurt. "You'll really like her. I mean—she's got this great red hair and these green eyes. And she—"

"Sara." Mom cuts me off. "Sweetheart. There's more. We could only get permission for *you* to see her, not us. One step at a time, remember?"

"Yes," I answer, barely above a whisper.

The visitor parking area at Maple View Center is nearly empty. We park and enter one of the buildings. The head of the center, a large man whose hair is as white as his coat, leads the Chandlers to an office and then motions for me to follow him down a long hall-way.

His voice echoes in the hall as he explains their procedure for visitations, how this one is special because it's my birthday and the Chandlers wanted me to have a special gift, and more things that I block out.

My thoughts turn to Anna. Will she recognize me? Will she remember I'm her sister? Does she still have Abby?

He opens a door to a room that has a wide mirror against the back wall. A table with four chairs sits in the middle of the room. Against another wall is a cream-colored couch, and a floor lamp stands beside it. Besides that, the room is empty.

"We had an incident with Anna just a bit ago," he says, motioning toward a chair. "This room is the lab where college students and parents can observe the behavior of the kids. Until I get clearance, I'll have to ask you to wait in here. Are you okay with that?"

I look through the mirror, searching for Anna, and nod.

A side door opens, and Anna walks in with an attendant. Anna doesn't see me, because of the special glass. I want to pound on it and call out her name, but I sit glued to the chair and stare. My sister blurs into a rainbow of colors. I wipe my eyes with my sleeve. Anna looks good.

Her hair has grown longer. It comes down to her chin. She's clutching Abby. An arm has been fashioned out of tinfoil to replace the missing one. I reach into my pocket and take out the real arm—something I carry with me everywhere—and prepare to give it to her. I notice she's wearing her half-heart necklace. I reach up and finger the other half on the chain around my neck, wanting to press them together like in the old days, when we played games and made promises.

The attendant says something quietly to Anna. Without warning, she whirls around and swings Abby, but the attendant is fast and catches the doll midswing. She pulls it from Anna's hand.

"No hitting, Anna. Use your words," the attendant says over and over. "Use your words. I have a very special surprise for you, but you have to use your words, Anna."

She circles Anna with her arms. Anna struggles, but the lady doesn't let go. A low, gritty, angry growl comes out of Anna. It grows louder and louder until it turns into a scream. I hold my hands over my ears, wishing I could comfort her and tell her everything is going to be okay. But it isn't okay.

When no more screams will come, Anna's mouth opens and closes soundlessly, like a fish. Her face is flushed, and her body droops over the nurse's arms. The lady looks over her shoulder and says to the glass, "We'll try this again when she's more ready." Within moments, the attendant that had let me into the lab shows up again.

"I'm so sorry," he says in a low, deep voice.

When I look through the glass again, I can see a shadowy image of myself, but I can also see through it to the observation room on the other side. It's as if I'm seeing myself actually standing in the room beside Anna. It's not the same as being with her, but it plants the image in my mind that I can memorize and picture long after I leave.

I hug my arms around myself to keep my thoughts steady. Anna is trying to get Abby from the supervisor.

"What do you have to do, Anna, to earn back your doll? Try to remember."

I feel an arm slip around my shoulders and look up to see Mrs. Chandler. "Are you okay?"

I nod, swallowing back a lump of hurt. Tears stream down my cheeks. I wipe my eyes and look back into the room where my sister sounds more animal than human.

"Someday, soon—" I start to say, then stop. *Words get broken,* Anna had said. I didn't want to make another promise I couldn't keep until I was sure. Until I was really, really sure I'd get to see my sister again. "At least she has Abby," I say, and sigh, hoping the doll is enough.

"And she has a lot of caring people around her to help her get past all the pain she has bottled up inside," Mrs. Chandler says quietly.

Kevin slips into the darkened room.

"That's your sister?" He presses his face against the window.

"Shhh." Mrs. Chandler pulls him into a hug. "Give Sara some space."

On the way back to the Chandlers', Kevin remains unusually quiet in the car. He reaches over and takes my hand, hugging it to him as he stares out the window.

"Thank you for taking me to see her," I blurt to Mrs. Chandler. "Do you think the center will give us another chance anytime soon?"

Mrs. Chandler takes in a deep breath and lets it out slowly before answering.

"Right now, it's all up to Anna, Sara. The doctors are worried about your safety and Anna's, and she has to go through the treatment program and prove she can manage her emotions."

"How long is the program?"

"Six months."

"Six months?" I say, louder than I mean to. "That's like forever."

"It feels like it, but when Anna gets through the program, she'll be able to visit with you, talk with you on the phone—"

Six months. Can Anna do it? Can I?

The thought gets caught in my throat. "Did Anna know I was there?"

"I think they were waiting to see how she behaved, Sara, before telling her, so no. I don't think she did."

Maybe that was better. I know if it had been me, and I found out I had missed a visit from her, I would be sick to my stomach.

Maybe not knowing was best.

CHAPTER 30

THAT NIGHT, I TOSS AND TURN. VOICES SLIP IN and out. I walk toward the voices and open a door into a room. No, into a garden. My new mom and Mrs. Craig are bent over something. I move up silently behind them.

"Is it a weed or a flower? I never can tell," Mrs. Craig is saying.

"It's beautiful, whatever it is," my new mom answers.

"But is it a weed or a flower?" Mrs. Craig repeats. She has a small garden hoe in her hand, ready to cut into the dirt and through the roots.

A new voice speaks. I can't see the face. "Weeds. Weeds. Too many weeds. Rip them out. Get rid of them. Weeds, weeds, too many weeds," the voice sings over and over, keeping a beat, like Mrs. Craig's garden hoe hacking at dirt.

I squint, trying to see the face, trying to match the voice to one I've heard before, and I groan.

"It's all right, Sara. I'm right here." I pull out of my dream and open my eyes. I see a shadowy figure sitting on the bed.

I can just make out Mrs. Chandler's face as she bends down and kisses me on the cheek. "It's okay, sweetheart. Everything is going to be okay. I know that you hoped seeing Anna would be different. In time, it will, Sara. In time. But now you must sleep. We're right here with you. Relax." Her hand brushes over my forehead.

I drift back to the garden. The ground around the remaining flowers is freshly churned. Holes gape where other flowers used to be. The flowers, deep red and purple, reach for the sun. I smell their light perfume. They smell like my new mom. My feet sink into the soft dirt. It covers my toes, rooting me.

Weed or flower? Weed or flower? A breeze blows through my hair. Weed or flower? I try to move but can't. Another voice, this one deeper. I try to place it. It's coming closer. What is it saying?

Let me put my arms around you. I can never live without you.

"Daddy!" I reach for the sky, my arms as thin as twigs. My hands are leaves waving in the wind.

"Daddy?" I force my eyes open.

"It's okay, Sara. You're safe. I'm here." A different face presses close to mine. I take in a deep breath and smell soap. Toothpaste. I look again. My new dad's face is smiling, but his eyes are scared. I see the fear in them as I'm pulled back into the garden.

"Rest, Sara. Mom and I are right here. We aren't going to let anything happen to you. Sleep."

The doorbell buzzes and buzzes. I jolt awake. In a chair beside my bed, my new dad sits up straight and rubs sleep from his tired eyes.

I frown. "How come—"

"The doctor gave us some medicine to give you, to help you rest. You cried out in your sleep, and your mom and I took turns staying with you," Dad explains.

I sit up and rub my aching head, then smooth out the blanket—a comforter covered with red and purple flowers, just like the garden in my dream. I hear the soft padding of feet coming up the stairs.

"Knock, knock." Mom grins sleepily at me from the door. "You have a visitor."

"Anna?" I jump out of bed and grab my robe, bumping against her on the way out. "Anna?" I race downstairs. But the visitor isn't Anna.

"Lexie. Hi." I force my face to look happy. Lexie is holding a box with holes in it.

"Hi, Sara. Can we talk?"

"Yeah, sure." I lead her up to my room. Mom and Dad pass us going down.

Mom sneezes.

"Bless you," we both say at once.

In my room, I curl up on the bed and pat a place beside me, just like I used to do with Anna. "What's in the box?"

Lexie sits, and a cat, meowing loudly, pushes against the lid of the box and then jumps out onto my bed.

"Sneaker!" I scoop her up and frown. "You're not going to tell me you're giving her away, are you?" I study Lexie's face for signs of bad news, but she shakes her head.

"No, no. It's not that." She takes a deep breath. "Our dads got together," she says, "and have helped Mrs. Craig get permission from the court to let Anna be part of a therapy program involving animals." She pauses to let the words sink in. "They've agreed to use pet therapy to try to help Anna with her problems"— Lexie hesitates—"instead of you."

"What do you mean, instead of me?"

Lexie shifts her weight. "I know you want to be with her, Sara, but I heard them say that she counted on you too much." Lexie stops talking long enough to give me room to cry.

I hug the cat. "Why'd you bring Snea—uh, Poof over?"

"I want you to have her. You can keep the box," Lexie says, sniffing loudly. "It'll make it easier to take her places."

"Really? You're giving her back?"

"That's what friends are for, right? To be there for each other? You found her first, so really, you should have been able to keep her."

Long after Lexie leaves, I cup the half-heart necklace in my hand and think about my sister with new hope.

Anna will have to learn how to behave better. That might take time. Maybe the time it takes will be the same amount of time I need to give her to grow.

Mom walks in holding a big, fat envelope.

"Lexie gave me Sneaker back," I say excitedly.

But something about the look on her face catches me off guard.

"What's wrong?" When she doesn't answer right away, a new panic zips through me. Something is terribly, terribly wrong.

CHAPTER 31

"I HAVE SOME NEWS THAT MIGHT BE HARD TO hear." She sits down beside me on the bed. Just the way she says it, the sharpened edge to her words, suggests that whatever she has to say can only be bad. "Mrs. Craig should be calling any minute."

"To take me away?"

Mom looks startled. "No, no, sweetheart. Nothing like that." She gives me a reassuring hug and then turns her attention back to the fat envelope. "It seems that your biological father has petitioned the court to keep you, blocking our efforts to adopt you."

"Biological." I hear the word a lot, but it never gets any warmer-sounding. It's cold. Like Daddy just made me and then disappeared. But that's not what happened at all.

"So, Anna and I get to go home?" I look up at her, surprised to see the hurt in her eyes.

"This is your home, Sara. I hoped you knew that and felt like we do. Your dad is back in jail. There's no way he can take care of you. He's doing this—" She turns her head. "First thing Monday, we need to go to court," she says, pushing away from the bed and stepping toward the door.

"What about school?"

"You'll just have to miss a day."

I shuffle downstairs, struggling with how my face should look. Sad because they're obviously upset? Or happy, like a tiny part of me is feeling because Daddy is still trying to get us back? Sneaker starts meowing, and I let her out of the box and onto the porch.

When I get back to the kitchen, the phone rings, making me jump. Mom talks for a moment, then hangs up and sighs. "That was Ruth. She says she'll meet us at the courthouse at nine on Monday."

"Do I have to go into court?"

"Yes, but I'll be in there with you."

"What about Daddy?"

"He'll be in court for the judge's decision."

Monday finally arrives. With Kevin at school, we start for the courthouse. The clouds above could easily be inside the car, for all the silence between us. The street turns from houses to gas stations to stores to office buildings, rising taller and taller. Then one street opens up to the courthouse, a huge building with arches and pillars standing guard. We park, and Dad takes my hand. He's shaking.

I look up into his face. He looks tired and older, his face broken by worry lines. I hug his arm.

We walk, the three of us, toward the steps that lead to the big glass doors.

Mrs. Craig waves to us from the top step. "You made it!" she says, forcing a smile and checking her watch. "Why don't you come inside?"

It seems like a strange thing to say, since we have nowhere else to go. We step into a large, echoey room that has shiny black-and-white squares on the floor. Like checkers, people move from one space to the next. We step through a security gate. The only alarms that go off are the ones in my heart.

Mrs. Craig leads us down a long, wide hallway to a carved wooden door at the end. There are benches along the wall. She sits on one and pats the seat beside her.

"Sara. Sit here for a moment. Let's talk before we go to see the judge."

I sit stiffly, keeping my back away from the wall, almost afraid to hear what she has to say.

"Your daddy's in there," she says, motioning toward the courtroom. "I must warn you. He has funny-looking clothes on, and he looks a lot different from when you saw him last."

I feel Mom sit down behind me, sandwiching me between herself and Mrs. Craig, but I don't look over at her. Dad, meanwhile, paces the floor, his eyes glued to the courtroom.

"Your father's going to try to talk the judge into letting him keep you," Mrs. Craig continues, "but he has to stay in jail for a long time this time, Sara, for child endangerment. It's going to be hard because I know he's going to plead with the judge to see you."

"What about what I want?" I ask.

She checks her watch again and glances at Mr. Chandler, nodding a quick nod.

"Sometimes grown-ups have to make the decisions, Sara. It's time to talk to the judge," she says.

My stomach tightens, and I'm torn between holding on to the bench, refusing to go, and facing the judge and his decision. "What do I say? Do I talk to Daddy too?"

Mrs. Craig shakes her head. "No, honey. Only the judge. He's probably going to ask you if you want to live with the Chandlers."

A tightness creeps up my neck, choking back tears. The Chandlers have been so good to me. But Daddy is *Daddy*. He's blood. He's family. What if something I say messes everything up? "You mean instead of living with Daddy?"

"Yes. Instead of living with your biological father," Mrs. Craig answers.

"What about Mama?"

Mrs. Craig sits up straight as a board. "Your mother has finally signed the papers giving the court permission to release you for adoption."

"Mama signed papers to give us away?" I slump against the back of the bench, feeling that hole of emptiness again that I felt when Mama first left.

Mrs. Craig nods.

"So, this means you know where Mama is?"

Mrs. Craig nods, glancing over my shoulder at Mrs. Chandler. "I'm sorry, Sara. We found her, and she has agreed that this is the best thing for you. A new home. A new start."

The wooden doors open, and a large man in a uniform tells us that it's time to go in.

"Are you ready?"

I shrug and follow. Mr. Chandler catches up and leans down close to my ear.

"We love you no matter what you say, Sara. We know this can't be easy."

I look back at the two of them and see the hurt in their faces. They hold each other while I walk into the courtroom with Mrs. Craig and head for the judge's chamber.

Alone is such a hard thing to be sometimes, and this is one of those times. I try to picture Lexie with me instead of Mrs. Craig, to see if that will help me calm down.

"What a kawinkeedink to see you here," she would say.

The judge's chamber is a small room that's full of books and smells like a library. A big desk sits like a gray boulder in the center of the room. There's a large chair, and in that large chair sits a large man draped in a black robe.

"Hi, Sara. I'm Judge Steinman. Do you know why you're here today?"

I stare at my shoes and nod.

"Decisions about who should raise a child are never easy. You have two loving people out there who want you as their daughter—and their son who wants you as his sister—not to be the daughter they never had, but to be the strong, brave girl you've become. And to have room to grow and play and be the child you are meant to be. I'm going to rule in favor of the Chandlers raising you. Your father is going to spend a few more years in jail. You need a family, Sara. Can you understand my decision?"

I look up at the round face behind the black robe and nod. He doesn't make me choose. The choice has already been made.

I stare at the pictures on his desk of his own family and nod again as I stand up from the chair. "Thank you."

The judge doesn't look happy about any of it either.

"Step outside and we'll call you into court shortly to hear my decision."

I guess in court you have to hear decisions more than once.

The Chandlers jump up the minute we walk out and rush over toward us.

Both are trembling. Their hugs feel real, and after some quiet talk with Mrs. Craig, all the worry lines in their faces have disappeared, replaced by looks of relief.

Mrs. Craig urges us toward the door and we step out into the echoey hall. While I bend to tie my shoe, Mrs. Craig draws them aside. "There's something I think you should know," she says in a low, official voice.

While they talk, someone opens the door to the court-room. One person comes out, and another goes in.

The one who sneaks in is me.

CHAPTER 32

THE CHURCHLIKE COURTROOM IS VERY QUIET. Wooden pews fill the center and face what looks almost like an altar. Up high, behind a looming wooden desk, sits Judge Steinman. I slide into a nearby pew and hunch down low, hoping he can't see me.

On one side of the judge is another row of seats facing sideways. There, chained to a group of men, is Daddy.

He hangs his head and doesn't look up when I stare at him. Mrs. Craig is right. He looks different without his hat and boots and jeans. He thrums his fingers nervously on the knees of his orange jumpsuit. Finally he turns his head and looks at me. His face is thinner than I remember. His cheekbones stand out, and his eyes look sunken and dark.

I bite the inside of my lip, trying to be the brave girl he taught me to be. I want to run over to him and tell him how sorry I am for getting us caught and how it is all my fault that they locked Anna up in that dumb residential center. I want to tell him that I wouldn't have gone to the 7-Eleven and stolen the paper towels if we'd had more to eat at home.

When he realizes it's me, his eyes light up. *I love you.* He mouths the words.

I was at the ocean once. It was so powerful, it scared me. We walked for miles on the beach, gathering shells and listening to the waves pound and then rush up to splash around our feet. The water was numbing cold. That's how cold my feet feel now.

"Court is in session, please rise," a man says, and everyone stands up. I look around and stand up with everyone else.

"You may sit," the low voice announces, and everyone sits, making a sound like pillows bumping.

The judge gives Daddy permission to talk.

"Please, Your Honor. If you'll just give me another chance. I love my kids."

I swallow hard. His words sound muffled and far away, as if I'm laying my head against his chest and hearing them from the inside out.

The judge says that while he feels sorry for Daddy's poor choices, he's had more than enough chances to turn his life around, and that we deserve to be in a home where we are safe and well cared for.

My head feels too heavy to lift, even though I know Daddy is looking at me. I know he's crying, too, because his voice sounds pinched and broken.

"Your Honor—" he begs.

Mrs. Craig's hands clamp on my shoulders. I barely feel myself stand as she leads me to the door. My legs are stiff wooden pegs.

"Let's go," she whispers.

The judge looks up and sees us and motions permission for us to leave.

I take one last look. Everything in me says to run— to find a hiding place, like I did for all of Anna's wet sheets, and wait for him.

No. No more running. I steal one more look at

Daddy. He slumps on the seat, looking like his heart has just broken in two.

Leaving the courthouse, I kind of know what it must feel like walking away from a cemetery. You know someone has died. You know they're buried. You know they won't just rise out of the earth and follow you, but something deep inside of you says that they can, and that they will, so you cling to that hope.

"Like I said, he's going to appeal," Mrs. Craig warns the Chandlers on the way out.

Appeal. A peel. I picture Mrs. Chandler's glass apple shattering.

"Who can blame him? If it were me, I'd be fighting with all I had to keep Sara," Mr. Chandler says, gluing the broken apple pieces back together again.

"I still love him," I blurt when we reach the car.

"We wouldn't have it any other way," my new mom answers. "I mean that, Sara. We're not trying to take you away from your mom and dad. We want to give you a home and be the family who can love and take care of you."

I believe her. "Do you think Daddy will ever get better?"

My new dad takes a deep breath and lets it out slowly as he gets in the car and buckles his seat belt. "I don't know if he'll get any better or not, Sara. A lot of times we learn from experience.

"Unfortunately," he adds, "some experiences are more painful than others." More belt buckles click, locking us all in.

We drive for a long time, with everyone deep in thought, but the deepest thoughts are buried inside me.

The sun beats warm against my cheek through the open window. Wind whips through my hair as I watch buildings flicker past. It's like seeing in reverse what I saw coming to the courthouse. I soon start to recognize stores, street signs, trees, and neighborhoods.

Except for that one awful time before Anna and I got split up, we had always been together, seeing the same thing. Now she's at the rehabilitation center going through big changes, and I'm an Olson-Chandler, trying to get the name to fit me and sound natural to my ears.

"Take time," Ben would say. And he's right. Not everything feels natural right away.

"Did I ever thank you for getting the rehab center to

say yes about Anna having a therapy animal to help her get better?" I ask, breaking the long silence.

Mom's shoulders relax as she glances at Dad and then turns to look at me over the seat. "Did we tell you that she might qualify for equine therapy?"

"What's that?"

"She'll get to work with horses."

"They'll let horses into the rehab center?"

They grin. "No, no horses in the center; she will get to go to the Center for Hope through Equestrian Therapy. There, Anna will be assigned a horse, and a therapist who can help her deal with her emotions."

I grin. "That sounds great, though I can't picture Anna on a horse."

"Little steps, Sara. They won't force her to do anything she doesn't want to do, but I bet she will want to ride and care for the horse, and that it will help her put everything into place," Dad says, when we reach our street.

"What a great day this is turning out to be," Mom adds.

I know I'll never stop thinking about Mama and Daddy, where they are and what they're doing. I know

I'll keep looking into faces I pass on the street, wondering if that's them and if they'll know it's me. But I also know as well as I know my name is now Sara Rose Olson-Chandler that my home is here, with my new family.

And maybe, someday, Anna will find a loving home too.

AUTHOR'S NOTE

GETTING SEPARATED FROM PARENTS AT AN EARLY age, and then getting separated from one's siblings, is something no child should ever have to experience. Some kids are lucky and are placed in loving foster homes, or adopted into caring families. Others are virtually left to fend for themselves.

The foster care system in our country is flawed. Caseworkers are given hundreds of cases to manage on no time and little pay, most doing what they can to help accommodate these displaced kids. Residence facilities are overcrowded. Certainly a lot has changed since I was in an orphanage and separated from my parents and siblings. Conditions have improved. But the fact is there are still kids having kids; parents incapable of or inexperienced with being effective parents; and angry, hurting, neglected kids trying to find their way through a maze of uncertainty.

I wrote *Sara Lost and Found* to share a little of my own personal experience, to give foster and adopted kids a voice, and to bring awareness to a painful abscess in our society that needs healing. It's not going to just go away. Look around. See what you can do to help. Become a Big Brother or Big Sister. Support programs that help kids through therapy. Look into fostering a child or adopting. Write. Educate. Open your hearts. Be part of the solution.

ACKNOWLEDGMENTS

MY DEEPEST GRATITUDE GOES FIRST AND FORE-most to God and my faithful guardian angels, who have always been there for me; to my incredible sons, Michael, Adam, and Jon; to my adoptive parents and brother, Ken, who bravely took on a feisty six-year-old so many years ago; and to my courageous siblings, Glenda, Harv, and Eileen, whose paths were anything but smooth. Heartfelt gratitude also goes to my first editor, Deke Castleman, who patiently worked through each paragraph, smoothing the bumps and nurturing the bruises; to Steve Mooser and Lin Oliver, for giving writers and illustrators the Society of Children's Book Writers and Illustrators (SCBWI), a sanctuary of

ACKNOWLEDGMENTS

support, connection, learning, and opportunity; to the Institute of Children's Literature, where I cut my teeth in editing and instruction; to Tom, Vicki, Judy, Sharon, Brooks, Gina, Gwyn, Kathy, Richard, Pat, Neil, Jay, Coni, and *all* my friends and colleagues who have been so supportive and encouraging; to Archway Publishing, which saw merit in the manuscript; and to Fiona Simpson, my editor at Aladdin and Simon & Schuster, for her keen eye, insightful comments, and belief in the importance of the topic.

With every beat of my heart, I thank you.

An unforgettable, inspiring story of hope and
innocence and one family's miraculous survival

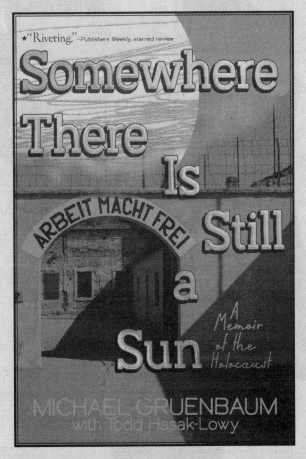

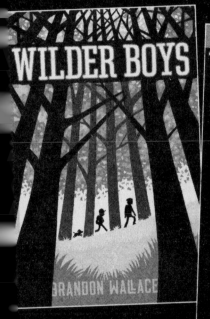

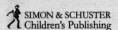